Comanche Territory

Chief Red Claw's Comanche renegades, supplied with the latest rifles by a greedy gunrunning outfit, are terrorizing settlers, burning, looting and killing. In desperation, the Army rehires former trail scout Clay Coleman, a man they once booted out for bending the rules. On the trail west, Clay rescues a mail order bride from a Comanche war party, then catches up with his old saddle partner, Shoshone Sam. Together, the two scouts match their wits and guns against Red Claw's warriors and the ruthless bunch of gunrunners. With the odds stacked against them, can they possibly bring peace to the frontier again? And can Clay survive to win the woman he loves?

Comanche Territoy

Cole Shelton

A Black Horse Western

ROBERT HALE

© Cole Shelton 2020
First published in Great Britain 2020

ISBN 978-0-7198-3113-3

The Crowood Press
The Stable Block
Crowood Lane
Ramsbury
Marlborough
Wiltshire SN8 2HR

www.bhwesterns.com

Robert Hale is an imprint
of The Crowood Press

Typeset by
Derek Doyle & Associates, Shaw Heath
Printed and bound in Great Britain by
4Bind Ltd, Stevenage, SG1 2XT

CHAPTER ONE

At first they saw the buzzards wheeling high in the azure sky, then as they crested the long, wooded ridge that formed a crumbling balcony over Seth McGrath's vast grassy valley, they made out little wisps of grey smoke curling ominously among the scavenger birds.

Lieutenant Peter Rawlings, riding just ahead of a dozen blue-uniformed cavalrymen, motioned to his sergeant, a lean rake from Missouri. Looking nervous at seeing the smoke too, Sergeant Buck Baker joined his lieutenant at the head of this small column sent out on patrol from Fort Adobe. They'd already come upon the charred bodies of two sodbusters beside the smoking ruins of their cabin halfway down Old Wagon Pass; now it was possible they were heading for yet another unwelcome discovery.

'Tell the men to ride slow, keep their eyes wide open and firearms ready,' the lieutenant told his sergeant.

'Yes, Lieutenant, sir,' Buck Baker responded with an army salute that seemed strangely unnecessary out here in the wilderness.

Rawlings slowed his brown gelding as Baker rode back down the line, relaying his orders in a soft voice just in case there were hostiles in the near vicinity. Riding ahead, as was his custom, Lieutenant Rawlings took a thin, winding trail across the sloping ridge. He led the way through flowering sagebrush, gave two clumps of grey rocks a wide berth, startled a mottled stag and headed to the line of cottonwoods that peered down over the valley where McGrath and his family had made their new home in the West.

That new home was now a blackened shell.

The cavalrymen sat saddle for a long moment, staring at the smoking remains of what had once been a three-roomed log home and stables.

Without a word being spoken, the riders followed Lieutenant Peter Rawlings down the wheel-rutted trail from the ridge. The smell of death and roasted flesh floated to them on the slight northerly wind blowing up from the valley floor. Rawlings had known this stench many times before, too many times.

 It never ceased to make his stomach turn.

He glanced back at Trooper Troy Grayson. He was barely seventeen, in the lieutenant's opinion far too young to be a soldier. The kid ought to be back home with his parents on their Missouri spread. Grayson's boyish face was already turning as white as his mother's flour. Then there was David Easton, not much older than Grayson. He'd joined the US Army to impress his father. He was more suited to punching cows like his brothers.

Rawlings reached the first body.

A slightly built man lay face down at the foot of the trail.

He'd been scalped and flies buzzed the mutilated crown of his head. A patch of matted blood lay over the clay earth under his neck.

As Lieutenant Rawlings expected, Grayson retched and spewed last night's supper into the dust. Trembling,

Easton deliberately looked away.

The lieutenant didn't reprimand the young bluecoat lads because he remembered his first time too.

Rawlings kept riding, leading his troopers past two other bodies, both men. He reined his horse a few paces from the smoking skeleton of what had once been a pioneer home. A larger body, scalped like the others, lay crumpled in the doorway. The face had been burned to a black mask, but Rawlings knew from his build he had to be Seth McGrath, a genial Scotsman who'd migrated to the New World to make a fresh start with his wife and three boys. By the sound of Sergeant Baker's hoarse cry of disgust, they'd just found Mrs McGrath. Glancing over to Baker, Lieutenant Rawlings saw the shreds of ripped and burned dress material clinging to a tuft of smoking grass just three paces from the woman's blackened, naked body. He wanted to throw up like young Grayson had.

The heat from the still-glowing timbers assailed Rawlings as finally he dismounted, scouted around the burnt walls and then beckoned Baker to join him. The two officers walked solemnly around the smoking ruins while their men kept in their saddles, guns ready, watching out in case the Indians returned.

And because the pioneers had been ruthlessly scalped, their killers had to be Indians, almost certainly Comanche renegades.

Mostly there had been peace between the Comanche Nation and white settlers, but one belligerent chief, Red Claw, had recently walked out of the tribal council and gathered together some restless, war-hungry warriors. Red Claw's rebel bunch was stirring up trouble all over this far frontier.

'No arrows,' Lieutenant Rawlings observed, casting his

7

eye over the remains of McGrath's ranch house. He used his knife to cut two slugs out of a charred window frame. 'Instead, bodies and walls riddled with lead.'

'Like at that sodbuster cabin in Old Wagon Pass,' Baker mentioned.

'And that way station attack Pat Perkins told us about,' the lieutenant was reminded.

'Yeah, damn blasted Comanches,' Sergeant Baker remembered what they'd heard. He folded his arms. 'Ole Pat Perkins and those stage passengers saw the raiding party. Half a dozen painted bucks, he said, but none of them shooting arrows. All with rifles. Perky was lucky those travellers in his way station were handy with guns so no one lost their hair.'

The lieutenant held up both bullets, asserting, 'These look familiar.'

'Same as what we found in Old Wagon Pass?'

'Rifle bullets.'

'Lieutenant!' It was Randy Baines, the oldest trooper on this patrol. He was once a Johnny Reb, but after the civil war ended, he switched uniforms. At first he was regarded with suspicion, but he was proving to be a good horse soldier so he was mostly accepted now. There was even talk he might become an officer one day. Pointing to the water troughs, he yelled, 'Lieutenant, over there! Another body!'

Lieutenant Rawlings and Sergeant Baker marched together across the blackened grass and halted by three water troughs. A young Comanche warrior lay sprawled between the two largest troughs, a bullet hole in his spine. When a battle was over, Comanches normally took their dead with them for traditional burial, so Rawlings surmised that after the raiders made their kill they'd left in a hurry. Maybe Comanche scouts had seen the troopers coming and warned the others to get out.

The Indian was still clutching a rifle.

'Springfield,' Rawlings said, easing the rifle from the Indian's death grip.

'Very latest, I reckon.'

Lieutenant Rawlings said nothing now as his eyes roved over the smouldering ruins of Seth McGrath's dream. Soon the troopers would bury that dream, dig five graves side by side near the cottonwoods that shaded the water troughs. They would bury the Indian warrior too, not next to the family, but somewhere behind the smoking remains of the stable. That would make eight graves they'd dug since leaving Fort Adobe on this patrol.

He knew for sure that Red Claw's renegades had at least some rifles. He had no way of telling how many. This meant someone, maybe a whole bunch of unscrupulous white men, were supplying those guns. They had to be stopped before more murder raids, or even an uprising took place and the whole frontier erupted.

Lieutenant Peter Rawlings looked north to the distant snow-capped peaks.

He figured there was one man the army needed right now.

Desperately needed, in fact.

He was a man many in Fort Adobe held in utter disdain.

His name was Clay Coleman and he lived far, far away in those mountains.

One week later, the first day of fall, Clay Coleman saddled Rusty, his chestnut horse, and left Beaver Town. He rode south through the mountains, followed the old trapper trail that clung to the mossy banks of Arkansas Creek, then spent an hour collecting supplies from Mike McPhee's Trading Post. After a good meal at Rose Marie's Eating House, he latched on to the winding trail that descended from the mountains and joined the road to Fort Adobe.

Clay Coleman was a tall man, head and shoulders above most. He had deep brown eyes, the kind that summed you up in a single glance. His nose was prominent, his lips firm, his chin strong and bold. Burning suns and freezing winds of a hundred trails had chiselled his face and hardened his skin so it looked like leather. He rarely visited Beaver Town's barber and his black hair reached down to the collar of his buckskin shirt. It wasn't easy to tell his age, but he'd be thirty-nine a fortnight before next Thanksgiving Day.

Now you wouldn't exactly call Clay Coleman handsome, but when he strode along the wooden boardwalks of Beaver Town, more than one woman would give him a wistful glance.

However, as yet Clay hadn't settled down, nor did he intend to.

Two days out from Beaver Town saw him on the rolling plains. It was familiar territory for Clay Coleman because he'd once been a trail scout here, riding with over fifty army patrols until that incident in Broken Bow. Even before that day he'd felt he was on borrowed time. Major Grant Keating, in charge of Fort Adobe, had never taken to him and when the military were informed about Broken Bow, the commander told him bluntly his scouting services were no longer required.

Clay hadn't argued. He'd grown tired of army discipline, which he was expected to obey or at least respect, even though he was a civilian.

10

And once he rode clear of Fort Adobe, he'd felt free.

He decided then and there he would never work for the army again – until he received the official letter that was folded in his top pocket.

Now, seven years later, he was on the way back.

Six days after leaving Beaver Town, Clay Coleman saw the walls of Fort Adobe. When the troopers first arrived here, they used adobe mud-bricks to build an outpost, hence giving the fort its name. Deciding to remain here, the soldiers erected a strong wooden stockade inside the original adobe walls. Now, as Clay Coleman rode closer, he saw the Union flag flapping at the top of the mast. There were two sentries on the eastern wall and when they saw the lone rider approaching they gave the order for the twin entrance gates to be opened.

He rode straight into the fort.

As he passed them, one sentry remarked to the other. 'Reckon that's Coleman!'

'You mean, Prairie Rat Coleman?' the second sentry sneered.

'I did hear the major wanted him back.'

'When Coleman left, I said good riddance. I still say it. We don't need the likes of bastards like him.'

The first sentry turned and yelled out for the gates to be closed. As he did so, he glimpsed something neither of them had noticed before. Small grey puffs of smoke were rising from a distant rim, half a day's ride west of the fort.

'Bastard or not, maybe we do need him, Trooper Smith,' he stated softly.

Clay rode across the dusty parade ground.

Not much had changed in seven years.

Soldiers stood in groups in the shade cast by the fort's stone barracks. A couple of troopers were playing cards.

11

Under the watchful eye of a snarling sergeant, half a dozen men were marching back and forth from the latrines to the eastern wall. Clay wondered of what minor misdemeanour they'd been found guilty. Maybe drinking too much alcohol. Reminded him of old times here when boredom often claimed half of Fort Adobe's bluecoats.

Smoke curled from a small fire beside an old chuck wagon.

Several soldiers recognized him as he rode further across the parade ground, casting a long shadow. One of them called his name. Another yelled out 'Injun Lover'. Clay took no notice.

Hardly giving the soldiers a second glance, Clay rode past them all and headed straight for Major Keating's office. It was still in the same place, right next to the officers' quarters.

Keating's obese adjutant, Johnson, who looked ten years older and whose flame-red hair was noticeably greying, sat reading a dime novel, smoking a cigarillo outside the office door.

Lounging next to Johnson was Frank Logan, a wiry, moustachioed trader, lean and hungry looking. Clay remembered Logan sure enough from his time here at the fort. He was still dressed in black. He'd never taken to Logan and as far as the trader was concerned, the feeling was mutual. They'd once had a fist fight when Clay had accused him of cheating in a poker game and Logan suffered a broken nose. In fact, there weren't too many who took to the trader. That hadn't stopped Major Keating's sister from marrying him because Logan could turn on the charm when it suited him. Being part of the major's family, Logan could take liberties like having his own rent-free storage room in the fort.

Seeing Clay ride across the parade ground, Logan had a brief word with Johnson, then stood up and deliberately walked away.

Looking up from his novel and seeing for himself that Clay Coleman was approaching, Johnson swore, scrambled to his feet, knocked on the door and turned its brass handle.

'Major Keating! Sir!'

'What is it?'

'Prairie Rat Coleman's here.'

'Go and fetch Lieutenant Rawlings – on the double.'

Dirk Johnson saluted. 'Yes, sir!'

Clay dismounted out front of the major's office and tied his horse to the hitching post. Major Keating was a wiry little soldier in his fifties who'd always resented being posted to this God-forsaken fort. A product of West Point, he'd always thought he was worthy of a more important appointment. However, being a professional soldier, he had to obey his superiors.

Now he sat waiting as his former chief scout entered his office.

The major was aware some had criticised him for terminating Clay Coleman's services but he'd stood doggedly by his decision. Despite this, he was determined to be cordial.

After all, he agreed with Lieutenant Rawlings. They needed him.

'Sit down, Coleman.'

Clay straddled the chair as Rawlings faced him over a mahogany desk piled high with papers that needed to be looked at – but who cared about paperwork in this frontier fort?

The lieutenant marched into the office to join them.

13

'Good to see you,' Rawlings greeted Clay amicably, bringing a frown to Major Keating's forehead.

'Same here,' Clay said.

'I'll come straight to the point, Coleman,' Major Keating said pompously, fingers stuck in the lapels of his blue officer's shirt. 'Once you disobeyed orders but that's in the past so I'll forget about what happened in Broken Bow.' His lips pressed together in a grim line. It was as if Keating didn't want to say what he needed to. However, after a long pause, the words spilled out. 'Fact is, the army needs help, Coleman, and Lieutenant Rawlings said you were the right man to ask.' Keating wrestled with himself before he finally admitted in a clipped voice, 'And I agree with him. The army and the settlers need your help.'

Clay frowned. 'The settlers?'

Lieutenant Rawlings explained. 'We have Comanche trouble, Clay, and settlers are getting butchered.'

Clay listened while Peter Rawlings told him about Red Claw's renegades and the indisputable fact that they were armed with shiny new Springfield rifles. Major Keating interjected by lamenting that some of the troopers in Fort Adobe hadn't even been supplied with these latest guns. Rawlings recounted the murder of settlers in Old Wagon Pass and McGrath's valley, the raid on Pat Perkins' Way Station and then recalled that only three days ago some troopers on patrol had just returned from a brief but fiery encounter with a Comanche raiding party south of Black Spear Creek.

In all instances, the Indians had carried Springfield rifles.

'Then there's the horse ranch,' Major Keating reminded his lieutenant.

Rawlings nodded. 'Two wranglers were murdered and

scalped on the Circle Three spread. I knew them both. Damn fine westerners. They were riddled with rifle bullets. Then, only last Sunday, a patrol saw a bunch of Comanches near the wagon trail used by settlers heading west. Every one of those Indians was armed with a rifle, so new the sun glinted on the metal barrels.'

'Someone must be supplying Red Claw with the latest Springfield rifles,' Major Keating summed up, 'and it's unlikely that filthy gunrunner could do it on his own. I'd say impossible. He has to have a bunch of white traitors in his pay.'

'But I don't understand,' Rawlings muttered, shaking his head in disbelief. 'Red Claw wouldn't have money to pay for toy guns, let alone real rifles.'

'But he has them, that's a fact,' the major said. 'None of us want to believe it, but possibly someone wants to deliberately start a Comanche uprising.'

'But for what purpose?' his lieutenant countered.

They watched Clay intently.

'So you reckon it's just Red Claw's renegades on the warpath?' Clay checked with them.

'The other tribes seem peaceful enough right now,' Keating affirmed. 'However, if this gunrunning outfit decides to supply Chief Long Knife's tribe, or even Chief War Bonnet's braves, then we'd have a wholesale Indian War on our hands. The whole frontier would be bathed in the blood of innocent settlers, not to mention young Comanche braves who'd get gunned down too. There'd be no winners in that kind of war.'

Clay asked, 'Have you any idea who these gunrunners are?'

'Not even the slightest notion,' Major Keating replied, shaking his head.

'No names come to mind,' Lieutenant Rawlings said ruefully.

'Fact is, Coleman, we've called you here to ask if you'd help,' Keating said, thrusting a fat cigar between his lips. 'Lieutenant Rawlings believes strongly you're the only man we know who could help us. He recommended me to write to you, regardless of the – uh – unfortunate Broken Bow incident and your subsequent dismissal.'

Rawlings turned to look straight at the former army scout. 'You know how to speak fluent Comanche. You can read Comanche trail sign like a book. You know Comanche ways. You can live for days away from towns, either in the mountains or on the plains. And you know how to handle a gun.'

'Makes you the best man to be trail scout for a dozen hand-picked cavalrymen, whose job it will be to unmask and eliminate the gunrunners and bring peace between Red Claw and the white settlers.' Major Grant Keating struck a match and lit his cigar, then raised his voice, 'It'll mean you re-signing on as a Fort Adobe scout for a week, a month, for as long as it takes. And because we find our-selves in a dire situation, I've been authorised by General Sangster to offer you triple pay. . . .'

During his ten years at Fort Adobe, Clay had earned forty a month, not always paid on time. It had depended largely on whether the Army pay clerk had received the government money. Now they were willing to pay a hundred and twenty dollars, money he could use right now as he'd been thinking about going into partnership with Trader Mike McPhee, setting up in Beaver Town.

However, the pay wasn't the only consideration.

'What do you say, Coleman?' the major wanted to know.

Clay thought about it some more as both military men

16

sat in silence awaiting his reply. Major Keating had little beads of sweat dribbling down over his forehead while Rawlings had his hands clasped, like he was praying. An ugly situation was brewing in Comanche Territory, so maybe he was.

'I'll take the job,' Clay said finally, 'but I won't be needing your soldiers to keep me company.' He saw Major Keating bristling, his face turning red. 'I'm certain you'd choose some good men to accompany me to make sure I do things by the Rule Book, but when I leave Fort Adobe, I'll be riding alone.'

'Coleman! For God's sake—' Keating blustered.

'Major, sir,' Lieutenant Rawlings restrained his superior officer. 'I trust Scout Coleman. I suggest we agree to his terms.'

The major stammered, his cigar falling from his lips, 'But – but how can one man – one solitary man – possibly bring gunrunners to justice and stop an Indian War?'

'If anyone can, this man can,' came the lieutenant's confident reply.

Muttering to himself, Keating retrieved his glowing cigar from his desk pad. He took two long puffs and glared at his former trail scout. He'd never liked Clay Coleman. In his view, Trail Scout Coleman needed more discipline. A week's marching around the parade ground would do him the world of good. In Keating's view, there was no place for a loner in the military.

On the other hand, Clay Coleman was a damn good scout.

He could read a trail like the back of a man's hand. He could follow unshod hoofs over solid rock. And he could talk to a Comanche in his own language. Now, on reflection, Major Keating told himself that maybe, just maybe, he should have turned a blind eye to that incident in Broken Bow.

'Lieutenant,' Major Keating said, flicking ash from his cigar, 'take Coleman to the quartermaster's store, let him take what supplies he needs, then escort him to the paymaster. I'm authorising two months' pay in advance.'

'Yes, sir,' Rawlings said.

'And Coleman . . .'

Clay stood up. 'Yes, Major?'

'The Army's relying on you. Best of luck.'

Clay didn't salute. He just nodded to Major Keating and followed Rawlings outside. He didn't need many supplies but he collected some spare ammunition for his old army rifle and Peacemaker Colt. He accompanied Rawlings to see Bill Davis, an elderly trooper who'd retired from active duty but stayed on in the fort dutifully manning the pay office. After his long spidery fingers counted out Clay's money, two hundred and forty dollars, Davis said in a whining tone that he hoped that Clay's services would be worth what he'd just been paid.

Davis too remembered Broken Bow.

The trail scout filled his canteens with water, mounted his chestnut and picked up his reins.

'There's something Major Keating didn't tell you,' Lieutenant Rawlings said. 'We still send a monthly patrol to Bitter Springs. There's just twenty, maybe thirty folks there counting a couple of half breeds and their kids. Scout Charlie Warren and a dozen troopers check that things are OK there. Thought it might be useful for you to know the army will be there – just in case you need us. The patrol leaves tomorrow at sun up.'

Clay recalled taking many patrols out there.

Bitter Springs was a half day out from Settler Creek on

the old Fort Buffalo trail. It was a sleepy community where nothing much happened, the whiskey was stale and the saloon girls well past their prime. He doubted whether anything much had changed. He doubted too whether he'd be needing Charlie Warren and his bluecoats. But there was someone else he had on his mind.

'So long, Peter,' Clay said simply.

Watched by a dozen troopers, he rode back across the dusty parade ground, through the open gates and headed west.

He didn't look back, but he heard the big wooden gates whine on their ancient hinges as they were closed shut and a heavy iron bolt drawn across. North of the trail he rode was high country, Comanche Territory. The same smoke signal that Clay had seen a full hour before the two sentries spotted it was still rising from the faraway ridge. Now, however, there was a second signal, this one much closer, less than an hour's ride. It was puffing from the bare rim less than a mile north of Lazy River Pass, which he intended to ride through.

Leaving the trail, aware of both smoke signals, Clay Coleman kept to timber cover as he rode Rusty, his chestnut horse, towards the mouth of the pass.

He couldn't see the lone shadowy figure who'd deliberately climbed up the ladder to the sentry's platform high on the western wall.

That man lit a cigarette and watched him ride all the way to the pass.

CHAPTER TWO

Clay Coleman knew Lazy River Pass well. It was narrow, shadowy, and hemmed in by sheer sandstone walls that overlooked a slowly flowing river that wound like an old dying snake across the boulder-strewn floor. He'd ridden this pass with over a dozen cavalry patrols during those years when he was on the Fort Adobe payroll, but never once had there been any trouble. In fact, the bluecoats had often made camp here beside the river, even caught fish in it.

But then, those were the days when there was relative peace between white settlers and Comanche braves.

Right now he rode Rusty slowly, weaving through timber as he approached the pass, but there was no way of telling whether the Indians sending up that smoke signal on that rim had seen him. Hopefully he would edge into Lazy River Pass without being spotted, but all the same, he kept looking up at the northern wall in case they were waiting in ambush.

He needed to go through this pass.

It opened out on a balcony ridge that overlooked the Plains Country he intended to cross because it was the quickest way to get to Settler Creek. There he hoped to catch up with Shoshone Sam, his old saddle partner, who like him used to ride for Fort Adobe. Now he might be called 'Shoshone' Sam but that was because he'd taken up with a squaw belonging to that tribe. Clay figured they would still be together, living in Settler Creek, the town Sam had headed for after unleashing a furious tirade at Major Keating for dismissing his fellow scout over the Broken Bow incident.

If any man on this far frontier knew anything about the gunrunners or had a suspicion who they were, it would be Shoshone Sam.

Clay intended to pay him a visit.

Besides, it would be good to catch up for old times' sake.

He rode deeper into the pass, halting to let his chestnut drink from one of the river pools. His keen eyes ranged over the high rims that hemmed in the pass. He saw no movement, no telltale glint of sun on rifle. He remembered there had been two smoke signals. He had also noticed another one floating from a high ridge way back from the Fort Adobe trail, however because of the soaring sandstone walls it was now lost from view. He slowed the chestnut to a walk and lifted his rifle as the river trail surged over the balcony ledge that presided over the rolling plains below. He drew the chestnut under a pecan tree and waited, listening, watching for five long minutes.

The smoke signal he was looking for no longer rose into the azure sky.

Below him stretched a silent land.

It looked peaceful, almost empty and it was crossed by a wheel-rutted wagon trail that meandered west to Settler Creek. Many times in the past, Clay and a cavalry column had rested horses right here and watched lines of distant horses and sometimes oxen pulling wagons covered with billowing white canvas, transporting pioneers on their way to a new life. There was also another trail, the one that led to Broken Bow.

Clay nudged his horse into a walk, riding down towards the plains country.

It was also Comanche Territory.

Previously when Clay rode for Fort Adobe, two Comanche tribes had their camps in the high country on the far side of the wagon trail. Another tribe lived mostly in the canyon country, much closer to Lazy River Pass. In the seven years since he'd ridden in these parts, some, if not all, could have moved their camps. He was sure Shoshone Sam would know.

By now the late afternoon sun was low in the western sky and shadows were lengthening over the plains. He rode past an arroyo, noting recent tracks left by unshod pony hoofs. Heading for the Settler Creek trail, he reached a bunch of cottonwoods on a lone ridge standing like sentinels in the prelude to dusk.

Emerging from the timber, he saw smoke.

It wasn't a smoke signal like the ones he'd seen earlier.

This smoke was curling and wisping into the fading sky.

Clay figured it came from a cooking fire. It could, of course, be a camp-fire lit by a lone traveller. From time to time, westerners rode alone across these rolling plains. However, it could be a Comanche fire. He decided to take a closer look, so he left the cottonwoods behind and rode his horse towards a large bald boulder that was perched on a rise overlooking the rising smoke.

He could smell the smoke now, even hear the crackle of wood in a fire.

Reaching the boulder, he drew his Peacemaker from its leather as he slid noiselessly from the saddle.

He inched around the boulder, standing motionless when he saw the camp below him. Sheltered by the rise Clay stood on, the night camp nestled in a hollow. Three Comanche braves, one a wizened old warrior with long scars across his chest, the other two much younger, probably in their twenties, stood around the freshly lit fire that was burning in a circle of small stones. The Indians were almost naked, bare-chested, wearing only breechcloths and moccasins.

They were laughing, nudging each other, making crude comments. Understanding nearly every word in the Comanche language, Clay knew exactly what they were jesting about.

Just beyond the fire, sprawled in the shadows cast by their pinto ponies, was a captive white woman. And she was almost naked, face down in the dry grass. There were ants crawling over the back of her neck. She only had strips of torn clothing clinging to her young body, barely covering her. Her hands were roped together, tied to a wooden stake thrust into the dirt. She had long hair the colour of ripened corn but like her young, squirming body, her tresses were smudged with dirt. Blood smudged the back of her legs.

Clay thumbed back the hammer of his gun.

Alerted by the sudden sound of a sharp metallic click, the Comanche warriors all looked up at the white man framed against the boulder.

The eldest warrior groped frantically for the rifle he'd left by his cloth saddle but Clay's Peacemaker snarled and the bullet bored into his chest, knocking him clean off his feet. Yelling, the Comanche warrior crumbled, dropped his gun and crashed headlong into the hot dust beside the cooking fire.

The other two braves ran for their guns, which leaned together against a cottonwood trunk. The tallest Comanche reached his rifle first. Seizing the gun with both hands, he spun around, but Clay was ready for him. Two Peacemaker bullets ripped almost simultaneously into the Indian's chest and he pitched sideways, plunging to the dirt beside the squirming white woman.

By now the third Comanche had his rifle blasting and his first bullet ricocheted from the boulder six inches from Clay's left hip. The Indian didn't get to take a second aim because Clay calmly fired a bullet that shattered his shoulder bone into fragments, then finished him off with another slug that thudded deep into his chest. He plunged dead to the ground.

Spooked by the sudden wild burst of gunfire, the white-eyed Comanche ponies surged against the two strands of rope that had been wrapped around some cottonwood trees to form a makeshift night corral. The top rope snapped under their impact and the ponies fled into the gathering dusk as Clay Coleman strode down the slope into the camp. Meanwhile, the woman had managed to turn on her side and Clay saw her frightened eyes, bloody nose and bruised cheeks.

Clay had just reached the fire when she screamed a frantic warning.

'Mister! Mister! Behind you!'

Clay wheeled around and glimpsed two Comanche riders, side by side on the far edge of the camp. He had one last bullet left in his Peacemaker, so he lifted his gun, but the Indians vanished like ghosts before he could shoot.

Moments later he heard the dull thudding of unshod hoofs.

Still holding his Peacemaker, Clay ran to the prisoner.

'Thank God, thank God,' she wept as Clay reached her.

Crouching down beside her, he unsheathed his hunting knife, bent over, lifted her two hands and slashed the rope that bound them. Flecks of grass and dirt fell away from the torn, ragged remains of her dress and also her body as she tried to sit up. At first the effort was too much and she flopped but Clay grabbed her shoulders and hauled her back up. The front of her dress and her bodice both hung in ribbons. She might as well be naked.

'Those two Comanches are sure to ride back and they may bring more with them,' Clay said as he pulled the woman to her feet. 'We're getting out of here.'

After all that time flat to the ground and roped to a stake, her body was still racked with pain and she felt dizzy. She struggled to stand upright and collapsed against him. Momentarily, Clay Coleman held her to him, while she drew new strength from him. She was sobbing, her whole body shaking.

Clay knew they shouldn't wait any longer.

He offered, 'If you can't walk, I'll carry you, ma'am.'

Fastening both hands around his left arm, the woman said tremblingly, 'I'll walk, Mister. Well, I'll try to—'

With her clutching hold of his arm, Clay climbed back up the slope.

He reached the big boulder and pulled her up next to him.

Clay heard distant hooting, like that of a night owl but he knew this owl was human.

Swiftly, he took her to his waiting chestnut. There he mounted the horse, reached down and lifted her up behind him. She wrapped her arms around his chest, holding him tightly as he rode away from the boulder.

It was sundown.

The western rims were etched starkly against the crimson sky and the night wind began to whisper over the sagebrush plains. Clay knew the woman needed clothes. She'd be feeling very vulnerable right now but his first concern was her safety. There were still two Comanche riders lurking out there so he needed to slip away as swiftly as he could. He wanted to ask her how she came to be in their hands, but not right now. Voices could carry in the deepening twilight. He felt the rise and fall of her young breasts against his back as she clung to him like she was clinging to life itself. She must have suffered a terrible ordeal and every now and then he heard her deep sobs.

With the sun almost lost behind the distant mountains, night closed in over Comanche Territory.

He halted his mount and listened for any sounds of pursuit. He heard nothing, not even a human owl. This was country he knew well so as darkness fell, he followed an arroyo, circled a hillock and found the cave he'd been heading towards.

With a last look over his shoulder, he climbed the rocky ledge to the entrance of the cave he and Shoshone Sam had sheltered in when they'd ridden for Fort Adobe. The cave yawned to greet him and he rode right inside. Once deep in the cave, Clay swung out of his saddle, then reached up to help the woman down. Gratefully, she placed hands on his strong shoulders and let him lift her to the ground.

'I'm going to stake out on that ledge outside the cave,' he told her. 'I need to make sure they're not on our trail. Meanwhile, you can open up my saddle roll. You'll find my spare shirt there. You're welcome to it. At least it'll cover more than that shredded dress does.'

26

'Thank you, Mister—'

'Coleman, Clay Coleman.'

Unsheathing his Springfield rifle from its saddle scabbard, he returned to the cave's entrance, leaving her to at least a semblance of privacy.

He stood outside on the ledge, motionless in the moonlight.

His experienced scout's eyes roved over the plains below, searching for the slightest movement. He glimpsed the faraway glow of the Comanche night camp-fire, still burning unattended.

But he saw nothing else.

Nevertheless, he waited outside the cave for a while, giving the woman time to change out of her ripped dress. Finding her tied up and almost naked, he knew full well what she'd been through. It wasn't the first time he'd been confronted with the fate of a white woman captured by Comanches. However, in his decade riding as a trail scout for the Army, he'd seen the other side too. Twice liquored up soldiers from Fort Adobe had raped Indian maidens, only to escape with a reprimand, even though their vile actions had endangered the peace between the Comanche Nation and the white settlers. Each time the army had sent him to talk to Chief Long Knife. His peacemaking missions had always had a good outcome, although last time Red Claw, the rebel who aspired to be chief of all the Comanche tribes, had spoken threateningly towards him at the council fire. He recalled thinking then that this upstart Comanche could well turn into a troublemaker.

Now it seemed Red Claw was leading a renegade bunch.

Springfield rifles in the hands of such men posed a

huge danger. The braves who'd captured the woman he'd rescued had all carried rifles. He was determined to find out who supplied them.

He heard her footfall from the cave.

Turning, he saw her standing in the entrance.

As he expected, the big spare shirt he carried was many sizes too big for her slim figure. She was swimming in it! In fact, it was so big and unflattering he couldn't even see her curves. The blue cotton shirt with a patch in the back just flopped from her slim shoulders to her knees. And yet, Clay told himself, she still looked attractive wearing this oversize, incongruous shirt.

'I'm Miss Abigale Wyatt,' she said softly, a tremor in her voice. She repeated, 'Thank you for what you did. You were very brave.'

'How did you fall into Comanche hands, Miss Wyatt?' he asked gently.

'I – I was travelling with some emigrants – on a wagon train,' she told him. 'There were nine wagons and we made night camp under a big rim. The trail scout, Mr Henderson, called it Rainbow Rim.' He knew the rim, named 'Rainbow' by enthusiastic Anabaptist missionaries thirty years ago. Abigale resumed, 'I went out of the wagon camp to fetch water from a creek. It was such a small walk – I thought I was safe. But – but they were waiting for me.' She swallowed deeply. 'All five of them.'

'You called for help?' Clay prompted.

Abigale shook her head. 'One of them, the old man, clapped a hand over my mouth before I could cry out. Then he stuffed some cloth into my mouth as they rode off with me. I almost choked, Mr Coleman. When they finally pulled the cloth out, I was too far away from the wagon trail for anyone to hear my screams. In fact, the

28

Indians just mocked me when I did scream.'

'How long ago did this all happen, ma'am?'

The tears were flowing again, flowing freely as she replied, 'I've spent three horrible nights as their prisoner.'

Clay was thinking that maybe the men of that wagon train were still looking for her around Rainbow Rim. If they'd heard no screams, perhaps they thought she'd fallen into the creek. He knew the creek that flowed under the Rim near the wagon trail; there were deep pools in it. It was possible for someone to drown in one of them. Then again, the wagon train's trail scout should have picked up the tracks left by the Indian ponies. Even now, they could well be searching the plains for her. It depended on the wagon-master. Some would agree to spend time hunting around for a lost emigrant, others would regretfully order an almost immediate resumption of the journey.

He asked, 'Where were the wagons headed for?'

'We were to call into Broken Bow for a few supplies, then on to our destination, Settler Creek.'

'Are your wagons pulled by oxen or horses?'

'Horses,' she said definitely.

'Assuming the emigrants spent one, maybe two days searching for you and then continued their trail, they'd be in Broken Bow about now,' Clay calculated. He decided, 'We'll start heading there at sun up, no trails, just a straight ride across the high plains country. Provided we don't run into Comanche trouble you could be reunited with your folks by sundown tomorrow.'

Abigale was silent for a long moment, staring at the dust by her bare feet.

Finally, she said, 'I'm very grateful for your help, Mr Coleman.'

'I need to stay here and keep watch for a while,' Clay

said. 'You go back inside the cave. You'll find some canned beef and a tin opener in my saddle-bag. Have yourself some grub and I'll join you soon.'

She nodded, turned and started to retreat back slowly into the darkness of the cavern.

Then he spoke. 'Ma'am.'

'Yes, Mr Coleman?'

'Was your whole family on the wagon train?'

'No,' she said, 'just my fiancé.'

'He'll be real pleased to see you, ma'am,' he tried to reassure her.

'I hope so – after what's happened,' Abigale said.

Clay recalled her tattered dress, her nakedness and the fact she'd been in Comanche hands for three nights. He knew what she meant. However, Clay told himself, if a man truly loved his woman. . . .

She interrupted his thoughts. Weeping again, she said, 'You see, Mr Coleman, I'm what is known as a "mail order bride". My fiancé, Mr Thomas Drury of Settler Creek, placed an advertisement in a Pennsylvania newspaper, which I answered. I never knew my father and my mother. They both died of cholera when I was fourteen years old. I was on my own and the letters Mr Drury wrote were certainly respectful. He sent me money for six stage coach journeys across America. The arrangement was for Mr Drury to meet me at Silver City where the stagecoach roads ended. And that's what happened. We met in the stage depot, had a cup of tea in Elva's Tea Room and thankfully he approved of me. He gave me a beautiful engagement ring. As agreed, we then started to travel together by wagon train to Settler Creek but on the way . . . well, you know what happened. . . .'

'Yes, ma'am.'

'I noticed you looked at my hand when I mentioned the engagement ring. I'm not wearing Mr Drury's ring because those – those Indians stole it, took it off me by force.' Softly, she added slowly, 'Like they took something else, by force.'

'Yes, ma'am, I understand and no one will be blaming you.'

'Are you sure, Mr Coleman?'

She broke off and ran back inside the cave.

Clay let her go. He stayed on the ledge and looked out into the darkness.

He could still make out the Comanche night fire but by now that was just a faint flicker. He walked along the ledge, checking the distant high country they would ride through tomorrow.

The wind was rising, whistling over the plains.

The only light now came from the ghostly full moon.

Satisfied they were safe for at least tonight, he returned to the cave.

Enough wan moonlight filtered inside for him to see her sitting on the dirt floor close to where Rusty was tethered to a needle rock. Abigale had found the single tin plate he carried and using the small food knife from his saddle-bag, she'd sliced the compressed beef into two shares. He figured she must be hungry, but she'd waited for him so they ate the small meal together in silence.

Until now, she hadn't asked him any questions but he noticed she'd been watching him closely. Despite Thomas Drury being on her mind, she wanted to know more about this rider who'd come from nowhere and risked his life to pluck her from the renegade Indians.

'I know nothing about you, Mr Coleman,' she ventured.

Clay wasn't a man for small talk. Even when he rode

with Shoshone Sam, who could yarn non-stop for an hour, he usually kept his thoughts to himself, not talking just for the sake of it. He was normally content with his own company but he decided he'd make an exception to his rule now. A woman who'd been through the kind of ordeal Abigale Wyatt had experienced needed to talk.

'I'm a trail scout, back working for the army,' he said.

He built a cigarette as he told her briefly how he'd come to be in Comanche country. She made the remark that she'd noticed her captors had the latest rifles and the oldest Indian had carved tribal symbols into his wooden stock.

She'd stopped crying by now but she was finding it hard to keep her eyes open.

'You look real weary, ma'am,' he remarked.

'I haven't slept for three nights,' she said.

'You can sleep now,' Clay said. He assured her, 'You're safe enough here with me.'

'Yes, Mr Coleman, I believe I am.'

Fleetingly she opened her eyes wide, then closed them. Clay fetched his saddle blanket and draped it over her sleeping form. Then he returned to the gaping mouth of the cave. Tonight he would not sleep. With his own Springfield by his side and his Peacemaker fully loaded, he began a lonely vigil as clouds edged slowly across the face of the moon.

Dawn brought moaning wind and driving rain from the north. Already creeks were racing, muddy water filled every arroyo and yesterday's tracks were virtually wiped out.

Leaving the cave at first light, Clay knew they wouldn't have to be concerned about any pursuit but they still had to watch out for Comanche riders stalking the plains.

Abigale had slept so soundly he'd had to wake her up and now she clung to him as he rode down the cave ledge and headed away.

They heard distant thunder and rain pelted them, soaking their clothes. After they rode through a rapidly rising creek, the chestnut's hoofs squelched in the new mud.

Late morning saw the storm pass and the sun break through clouds.

They headed through Old Wagon Pass and Clay reined his horse momentarily to look at the charred walls of the Denver cabin. It was just a blackened skeleton, silent, forbidding, originally raised by Leonard and Phoebe Denver, whom he'd known. More than once Clay, Shoshone Sam and the troopers on patrol had been billeted here overnight. Back then, Chief Long Knife had been undisputed Comanche leader and there had been peace and trade between white settlers and the Indian Nation. Now wet stones marked the two graves that Major Keating told him had just been dug by his troopers. Clay felt angry. Leonard and Phoebe had been decent, honest folks, the salt of the earth.

Later in the day he came upon the remains of the McGrath home. He spent a few moments lingering by the freshly dug graves. He'd known the McGraths well too. He recalled that Mrs McGrath had once made coffee and baked cookies for his entire patrol.

Why in hell would Red Claw want to murder decent folks like these who'd never sought to steal, rape or dispossess them of their land?

Maybe possessing the latest rifles had gone to the renegade chief's head.

The gunrunners had to be stopped.

Two hours later Clay and Abigale reached the wagon trail.

There were many wheel marks in the mud but Clay managed to pick out some that had been made recently, almost certainly in the last couple of days. Maybe he would catch up with the emigrants in Broken Bow, reuniting Abigale with her man.

He had the thought, which he wouldn't share with her, that if she was his woman, he'd still be back on the trail searching, hunting for her.

Perhaps Thomas Drury was.

Clay followed the wagon trail across a flat grassy plain.

The trail mounted a long rise, then slewed down into Broken Bow. As he crested the rise, Clay Coleman saw the small town below, a settlement of clapboard and log buildings on either side of a dusty street. Just beyond the town was a river that curled across open range.

He saw no wagons so he figured the emigrants either hadn't arrived yet or they'd bought their supplies and left for Settler Creek.

Instinctively, his eyes were drawn to the tall pine they would soon be riding past on their way in. It cast a long shadow over the trail.

It was the town's hanging tree.

CHAPTER THREE

The sign was painted red, nailed to an old stump, announcing 'BROKEN BOW WELCOMES WAGON TRAINS'. He'd ridden past that sign many times before. They might embrace emigrants who'd spend money in their town but he wouldn't be welcome. The incident at Broken Bow might have taken place seven years ago, but he figured some folks at least would have long memories of what happened at the hanging tree.

Clay Coleman drew adjacent to the tree now.

He glanced up at the pine tree's high branch where they threw the hanging rope over. He saw the notch where one end was secured tight. The deep shoe marks made by the saloon keeper's big horse upon which they always sat the prisoner to be executed were clearly etched into the ground. The unfortunate man about to be hanged would listen to prayers recited by lean, grim-faced Reverend Cummings and then the horse would be slowly led forward, leaving the prisoner dangling, dancing rope until his neck snapped.

But there was one early morning execution that didn't take place.

Riding past the hanging tree, Clay recalled what happened like it was only yesterday. A young Comanche buck named Isatai, barely sixteen years old, had been caught red-handed stealing food and a blanket from Morgan's Store. At the time there was no sheriff, not even a deputy, in Broken Bow, so when Buck Morgan proclaimed in his raucous voice, 'all thievin' Injuns need to be taught a lesson', saloon owner Rob Trapp chimed in by declaring it was a 'damn good time for a legal execution'. Clay had ridden into the settlement just in time to see the young Comanche lad sitting white-eyed and terror-stricken on Morgan's horse. Saloon man Trapp was smoking a fat cigar, smoke curling past his thin black eyes. There was a noose tightened around the young Comanche's neck and he had moments to live. Clay heard Reverend Cummings declare the boy was a pagan so he wouldn't bother reading from the Good Book. They might as well hang the young varmint now and get it over with. Trapp chimed in with, 'Once he's dead, it'll be drinks on the house.'

And that's when, seven years ago, army scout Clay Coleman had reached for his Peacemaker and spoiled the neck-tie party.

Right now, Clay and Abigale left the hanging tree behind and rode past half a dozen clapboard houses. Being late afternoon, Broken Bow's street was almost deserted. It was like the town was sleeping. The red-faced barber sitting out front of his shop smoking a pipe and two women in long grey dresses talking outside the stone walls of the Broken Bow Gospel Church were the only folks he could see. The women had already spotted him riding into town and by the looks on their faces they were already discussing the spectacle of a young woman wearing a man's shirt with her bare legs dangling either

36

side of the horse's back.

Clay slowed his chestnut.

'Ma'am,' he said, riding to the store's hitching post, 'Buck Morgan and I don't see eye-to-eye but that won't stop him taking my money. We'll go inside, so you can fix yourself up with some decent riding clothes.'

'You've done enough for me, Mr Coleman,' she protested.

Clay said, 'As you can see, your wagons aren't here. Could be they'll roll in real soon, or maybe they've left and they're on the trail to Settler Creek. Either way you'll be meeting up with your Mr Drury real soon.' He added, 'I don't think you'll want him to see you like you are now.'

Abigale looked over at the two whispering women, whose faces wore shocked expressions. The old barber had seen her too and his eyes were suddenly popping wide, almost out of their sockets. It wasn't every day he saw a woman swimming in a man's shirt on the town street.

'I'll make sure Mr Drury pays you back for every last cent you spent on me,' Abigale declared.

'Go into the store before it closes,' he advised.

'Yes, thank you,' she said, sliding from the chestnut's back.

Clay tied the horse to the hitching post while Abigale wove her way between the bags of flour, barrels of redeye whiskey and racks of men's pants littering the boardwalk, finally entering Morgan's Store.

Wanting to give her some privacy in selecting women's clothing, the trail scout smoked a cigarette outside. He saw the barber, Preacher Cummings, Trapp and two others gather in a group out the front of the saloon.

Just a cursory glance at these men told him they still remembered the burst of gunfire under the hanging tree.

Clay finished his cigarette and went into the store.

'Hell's fires! Injun-Lover Coleman!' Morgan spat out his disgust as he saw Clay walking inside. He mumbled to no one in particular. 'Didn't think you'd have the damn nerve to show your face in here!'

Ignoring the storekeeper's tirade, Clay stood smiling, appraising Abigale Wyatt who'd just emerged from behind a thick red curtain, now dressed in the new clothes she'd chosen – light blue cotton blouse, fringed buckskin pants, black boots, all serviceable for riding the plains. She had his shirt neatly folded over her arm.

'I picked some undergarments too,' she said very confidentially to Clay. 'Hope you don't mind?'

'That's fine, ma'am,' he said.

He was watching Buck Morgan closely. Broken Bow's storekeeper had doubled as the town hangman for a decade. He was a cold-eyed, long-nosed former soldier who'd once served at Fort Adobe but had been booted out for undisciplined behaviour. Later, Morgan had been the main complainant against trail scout Coleman. Now his face was a mask of hatred, the same as it had been under the hanging tree. His right wrist, shattered by Clay's bullet, still dangled uselessly but his left hand was just inches from his holstered Colt .45. His wife, thin as a rake and dressed in black, grabbed that left hand, restraining him.

'How much does the lady owe you?' Clay demanded.

'The blouse was made by a decent Christian white woman to raise money for our Gospel Church Temperance Society, the trousers and boots came from the Western Frontier Clothing Company and as for what your lady friend is wearing underneath, I made them myself,' Mrs Morgan said. She decided, 'We'll take fifteen dollars for the lot.'

Preacher Cummings, Trapp and a rather nervous barber filed into the store behind Clay and Abigale. A quick glance showed Clay that Trapp held a rifle. He was smoking a cigar, just like he had seven years ago and his eyes were just as dark. Another townsman shuffled inside. He was Derick Burgan, shaggy-bearded, built like a buffalo, a former gold prospector who'd hung up his pan and retired here in Broken Bow. He was a man of few words and he stood with his back to the wall watching and listening as Clay counted out the money and placed the correct amount on the counter. It was Mrs Morgan who scraped the dollars in with her veined hands and stuffed the cash into their money box.

'So what are you doing back here?' the preacher snapped.

'Working for Fort Adobe.'

'What!'

'Some ornery skunks are supplying Red Claw with rifles,' Clay told them, standing alongside Abigale. 'I aim to stop them.' He looked around at them, one by one, as he said, 'So if anyone in this store knows anything or has heard anything about gunrunning, I want to know.'

Cummings raised his voice, like he was preaching a sermon. 'I'm sure Major Keating had the best of intentions in hiring you but in my view a man who intervened in a legal execution of a heathen Indian and then blatantly shot a decent citizen like Mr Morgan, robbing him of the use of one arm forever, isn't fit to ride for the United States Army.'

'Yeah, get out of our town, Coleman,' Burgan told him bluntly. 'And good riddance!'

'Well said, Mr Burgan,' the preacher applauded enthusiastically.

'As for you, woman,' Mrs Morgan called out to Abigale, 'don't lower your standards by settling for trash like him. Instead, get yourself a decent man.'

Abigale, flushing slightly after being mistaken as Clay Coleman's woman, stood firmly beside the trail scout. And she didn't intend to budge either.

But then Clay told Abigale quietly, 'Wait for me outside on the boardwalk, ma'am.'

'Yes, Mr Coleman,' she said, starting to feel more nervous with every passing moment.

She backed outside but kept looking through the open door.

The trail scout faced his hostile accusers.

'Sure I stood in your way and the Indian lad rode free,' he reminded them. 'I've said this before and I'll say it for the last time again. It was a freezing winter, there was snow on the ground. The buffalo had gone south, there were hardly any deer. The Plains Indians were starving and that young buck who snuck into your town was a Comanche kid wanting food for his family.'

Clay knew they were still unimpressed.

'That doesn't excuse blatant theft,' the town preacher said. He quoted belligerently, 'Thou shalt not steal. That's the seventh commandment.'

Clay turned his attention to the church pastor. 'I'm not a religious man, Preacher Cummings, but my pa used to read from the Good Book at the table after supper and from what I remember, we're supposed to feed the hungry, not string up their kids.'

He paused as Reverend Cummings bristled crimson with rage.

'Don't you preach to me,' the preacher fumed.

'Reckon it's a sermon you all needed to hear,' Clay said.

40

They all stared at him with hostile eyes. Morgan's left hand was itching to swoop. Burgan and Trapp looked like a couple of dangerous sidewinders ready to strike. The barber was simply trembling like a leaf on a windy day.

Clay addressed them all slowly in a tone that was cold as winter's ice. 'Now, I'm going to take Miss Wyatt over to Blacksmith Alden's place and see what horses he has for sale, so hear this, all of you. Unless you have some information on who's selling rifles to the Comanches, stay out of my way.'

He fixed his steely eyes on Morgan, watching as the storekeeper edged his left hand well clear of his gun. Then he looked straight at Trapp, who shrugged, then slowly lowered his rifle, finally resting it over a bag of flour. Derick Burgan didn't seem to be wearing a gun but all the same, he kept his hands where Clay could plainly see them.

'I'm glad we all understand each other,' Clay Coleman said. 'Let's keep it that way.'

He backed to the door and joined Abigale on the boardwalk.

Leading his chestnut, Clay walked beside Abigale, heading down the street past the barber's shop and the six dusty windows of the Last Deuce Card House. He glanced back over his shoulder once. The men who'd been crowding him in Morgan's Store now stood in a bunch watching him.

Sure, they detested him.

Broken Bow was a small community, no sheriff, no judge and they made their own law – a suspect held at gunpoint, a hasty 'justice meeting' in the saloon, a very prompt verdict, then a punishment to fit the crime. Mostly punishments ranged from a night in the crude makeshift prison cell built behind Morgan's Store to a pistol whipping. Criminals convicted of more heinous crimes were usually dragged or frog-marched to the hanging tree.

The blacksmith's forge was at the far end of the street.

Jonathon Alden was one of the more genial members of the Broken Bow community and he remembered Clay from the times he'd ridden in with troopers from Fort Adobe. In fact, he'd made some tidy sums of money re-shoeing their horses. As Clay and Abigale approached, Alden looked up from hammering a glowing hot horse-shoe.

'Trail scout Coleman with a real pretty gal,' Alden greeted. He chuckled as he dropped the horseshoe into a bucket of cold water, making steam billow into the air. 'About flamin' time too.'

Clay didn't spend time explaining that Abigale Wyatt, whose cheeks flushed slightly pink, didn't actually belong to him.

Instead, he returned the blacksmith's amicable greeting and pointed to the three horses grazing in the corral behind his forge. Two were spirited geldings, the other a more docile-looking black mare. The same hand-painted 'HOSSES FOR SALE' sign that had been nailed to the gate seven years ago was still there today, faded, weather-beaten, but firmly in place.

Clay walked across the corral and checked the black horse.

'How much for this mare?'

'With saddle?'

'Yes,' Clay confirmed.

'Twenty bucks,' Blacksmith Alden decided. He added, 'It's a fair price. Quiet, peaceful, perfect for a woman. Doesn't buck, doesn't bite.' He scrutinised Abigale before declaring, 'Good hoss for a beginner.'

Clay told him, 'I'll take the mare.'

Always the salesman, Alden complimented the buyer. 'Excellent choice, Mr Coleman.'

The blacksmith smoked a pipe as Clay counted out the money.

The scout asked, 'When were the last emigrant wagons in town?'

'Two days ago,' Alden said. 'That ornery old scout, Jasper Studebaker, brought 'em in. Only stayed an hour, enough to collect supplies and for me to shoe Jasper's old grey nag.' He scratched his itchy head. 'They seemed in a hurry to get to Settler Creek.'

Clay saw Abigale lower her eyes. He knew what she was thinking, same as he was. The emigrants can't have spent much time looking for her in the wilderness. That was unless her bridegroom-to-be, Mr Drury, was still out there diligently searching for his mail order bride. Unlikely, Clay thought, especially as he'd be on his own.

However, Clay knew some men who'd spend days, weeks, even longer, searching for a lost woman like Abigale Wyatt. He certainly would.

Ten minutes later, Clay and Abigale rode out of town.

They didn't notice a furtive hand draw curtains to one side.

Neither did they see the pair of flinty eyes watching them leave the town limits and take the emigrant wagon trail to Settler Creek.

Once they were out of sight, the watcher at the window shrugged into his old southern army coat, then reached for his rifle and ammunition. He walked to the livery stable and took his time saddling his shaggy mustang.

There was no hurry.

He'd smoke a couple of cigarettes first, maybe have a drink and then head out of Broken Bow.

It would be a good night for a killing.

Clay and Abigale rode west together without needing to rest their horses. The mare that carried Abigale lived up to Alden's prediction – suitably quiet for a woman who was unused to being in the saddle. And, Abigale confirmed to Clay as they left Broken Bow behind, this was the first time she'd ever ridden a horse on her own. She'd been a city girl all her life.

Upon hearing this, Clay rode at walking pace.

Tomorrow, when she was more confident, he decided they'd ride faster.

For now, he was content for them to take their time while he kept his eye on the distant high rims and ridges that overlooked the westward trail.

He saw no smoke, no Comanche riders, not even any raised dust as they followed the recent wagon wheel tracks over the plains. They rode by Sagebrush Pass with its low, crumbling walls of granite and as the day came to a close, they forded the shallow Two Arrows River and barged through tall reeds to mount the far bank.

Sundown was a crimson sash across the far western rims and dusk closed around them like a shroud. Clay circled a small buffalo herd and led the way down into a wooded hollow where he'd often spent the night beside a camp-fire with Shoshone Sam and a dozen cavalrymen on patrol.

Only tonight he'd light no fire.

While Clay secured their horses, Abigale prepared cold cooked bacon, dried fruit and molasses.

'The blacksmith said the wagons are two days along the

44

Settler Creek trail,' Clay stated as they ate supper. 'We'll be moving faster than wagons so we might well catch up with the emigrants by this time tomorrow.'

'That – that will be good,' she said.

'And you'll be reunited with your Mr Drury.'

'Well, yes,' Abigale responded uneasily. She raised her eyes and looked directly at him. She lowered her voice to a soft whisper. 'And he'll want to know what happened.'

'I guess any man would,' he agreed.

Abigale was silent for a long moment.

Finally, she said, 'It won't be easy to tell him.'

'Ma'am—'

'I'd like you to call me Abigale,' she said suddenly.

'Be pleased to,' he said.

She asked boldly, 'And may I call you Clay?'

'Sure.'

It seemed odd that she continually referred to her fiancé as 'Mr Drury' when she had just asked to call him by his first name but Clay kept his thoughts to himself. Maybe this Mr Drury was one of these very 'formal gentlemen of means'.

She was hesitant. 'May I ask you something personal, Clay?'

He nodded. 'Fine by me, Abigale.'

'If you had a woman who was captured by Comanches, would you – would you – still want to—?'

It was then, quite suddenly, that Clay heard what sounded like the sharp snap of a twig.

He looked up over Abigale's shoulder and caught a fleeting glimpse of a grey shadow slinking furtively along the eastern crest of the hollow behind them.

Instinctively, Clay reached over, grabbed Abigale's arms and pulled her to the ground beside him. Moments later,

45

a gun thundered from the darkness and two bullets thudded into the earth inches from her left leg. Clay lifted his Peacemaker and fired a quick shot at the looming shadow as another bullet from the rim smacked into their tin plate, sending it spinning.

'Keep down! Stay low!' he told Abigale.

Crouching, Clay fired another bullet at the elusive moving target, then he ran to the far side of the hollow and began to climb the slight slope.

He reached the top and saw the figure of a man, stark and black against the moon, standing to his full height now, hovering over their camp.

Clay's command cut like a knife. 'Drop that rifle!'

Fleetingly, the man simply stood like he was pegged to the ground, but then he swung around, rifle blazing. Clay's Peacemaker blasted a single bullet deep into his chest and he folded over his smoking gun. Then he crashed headlong into a clump of ryegrass.

Warily, Clay approached him.

The man lay still as a stone as the trail scout bent over, took a Springfield rifle from his claw-like fingers and turned him face up to the rising moon.

The dead man was Derick Burgan, the burly, bearded one-time gold prospector who'd been in Morgan's Store.

Clay checked their back trail and saw no movement. Burgan looked to have come alone. But why did he do this? Surely it wasn't over that incident seven years ago? He knew the town was still angry, but were the folks so unforgiving they'd send one of their own out into the night to kill him? Somehow he doubted it.

He figured Burgan had done this on his own account. But why?

46

Clay headed down to where Abigale was still flat to the ground.

He helped her to her feet.

'I'll bury him and we'll ride out of here,' he told her. 'Those gunshots might bring other unwelcome visitors.'

Knowing he meant Comanche braves, Abigale trembled in fear at the very thought, the terrible memories returning like a dark, evil tide as she clung to him.

He removed her clutching hands from his arms, fetched a prospector's shovel hanging in a sheath from Burgan's saddle and started digging the ambusher's lonely grave.

Night owls hooted and distant coyotes barked.

Then all was silent as Clay shovelled earth over Burgan's still-warm body.

Within ten minutes Clay and Abigale rode into the bleak wind sweeping across the lonely plains.

CHAPTER FOUR

Dark clouds made a dense canopy over the wilderness and a few spots of rain pocked the trail dust as the two riders followed the wagon trail across the plains. It was late in the day when Clay first spotted wagons stirring up dust at the foot of a distant mesa. He reined his chestnut, sitting saddle as Abigale, now riding her mare as well as most cowpokes, came alongside him.

'They're two hours ahead of us,' he told her. 'Should catch up with them by the time they form the night circle.'

Abigale nodded, saying nothing, thinking about her reunion with Mr Drury. Her eyes dropped down to her clothes. Mr Drury would remember her in a dress. It was a dress he'd bought for her in Silver City, the same hour he'd given her that engagement ring. Now the dress lay in grubby, bloody tatters on the plains and her ring, well, she had no idea which Comanche had ripped it from her finger. In their haste to ride clear of the Indian camp, there had been no time for her to search around.

Clay lit a cigarette, his eyes narrowing as they followed the lead wagon.

She caught his frown. 'Is something wrong?'

'I reckon they're turning off the main trail,' Clay

observed. White canvas, like faraway sails on a sea, looked to be heading off course, deliberately away from a sagebrush flat the emigrants usually crossed. 'Looks like they're heading north for some reason.' He turned to her. 'Did you say your scout was Henderson?'

'Yes, Mr Lucas Henderson,' she confirmed.

'Heard of him,' Clay said quietly.

Although he'd never met Henderson while scouting for Fort Adobe, he remembered camp-fire talk about the man who used to guide emigrants along the Oregon Trail. Apparently, Henderson had all the credentials to be a good trail scout but in the past Clay had listened to stories that concerned him, like his supposed midnight rape of an emigrant widow and his pistol-whipping of an unarmed, elderly Mexican to whom he'd taken a dislike.

'He only spoke to me once or twice,' Abigale remarked. She recalled, 'Mostly, though, I was with Mr Drury, who hardly let me out of his sight, except for that time I went for that walk to the creek.'

Clay drew on his cigarette, watching the line of billowing canvas slip past the towering mesa into the gaping mouth of Rattlesnake Pass. He noticed the last wagon lagged behind the rest.

What in the hell was Henderson doing?

He flicked his cigarette into the dust and picked up his reins.

'Stay close,' he told her.

They headed across the flat plain, forded a shallow river and reached the shadows of the mesa as dusk closed around them like a shroud. Sagebrush lashed their horses as they rounded the mesa and reached the rugged entrance of the pass.

He saw no wagons.

Henderson must have taken his charges deep into the passage.

Clay kept one hand on his rifle as he followed the fresh wagon wheel tracks in the soft dirt. The wind filled Rattlesnake Pass with ghostly whispers. The high walls blocked out the last light of day and lone pines cast long shadows. The grassy floor sloped down as the pass widened.

It wouldn't have been easy to take the wagons this far into the pass but suddenly Clay Coleman saw them.

They were just below them, formed in a circle, nine emigrant wagons bound for Settler Creek. Someone had lit a fire in the middle of the camp and its light flickered over womenfolk and cooking pots. Two young women were carrying water buckets from a creek. Clay saw three men drinking by the fire while others secured horses inside a hastily erected corral.

He nudged his chestnut into a walk and together with Abigale, he rode down the slope. There seemed to be no sentries because no one noticed them until they reached the circle and rode through the gap between two covered wagons.

'Can you see your Mr Drury?' he asked.

'Yes, I can see him,' Abigale replied. 'He's that tall man in the dark suit talking to – to the widow woman, Avis Whitely.'

Thomas Drury did indeed look like a gentleman of means, Clay observed, dressed immaculately like he was going to a dinner rather than getting ready for a wagon camp supper. Tall and lanky, he looked to be at least twenty years older than his mail order bride.

Clay and Abigale were inside the wagon camp now.

It was Drury himself who saw them first, initially calling

out a warning that strangers were entering the wagon circle, then simply standing there motionless and speechless as he stared at the incoming female rider.

Clay and his companion rode further into the firelight.

The emigrants called to each other, women looked up from their cooking, children stopped playing 'Hide the Thimble' by a big Conestoga wagon and men who'd been settling the horses down for the night strolled back into the circle.

'Miss Wyatt!' Drury finally broke his silence. He was staring incredulously at his mail order bride. Then he blurted out, 'You – you're safe!'

'Yes, thanks to this man, Clay Coleman,' Abigale said.

Thomas Drury didn't move, still standing alongside the white-faced young widow as Abigale slipped out of her saddle. Finally, however, he spoke a brief word to Avis Whitely, who put her hands on her hips as he walked towards the woman he'd promised to marry.

'What happened, Miss Wyatt?' Drury demanded.

'Comanches took me, Mr Drury,' she said.

He halted then and let her approach him slowly. 'Yes, yes, I realize that. We all did.' He reprimanded her sternly, 'You were foolish to fetch water on your own, Miss Wyatt. Very foolish indeed. Some of the good emigrants here lost a lot of sleep. In fact, they spent half the night looking for you.'

'Sorry to have caused so much trouble, Mr Drury,' Abigale said softly, reaching tentatively for him.

'In fact, some of us went searching at daybreak,' Drury told her, standing stiffly as she sought unsuccessfully to grab hold of his hand. 'Of course, we had to break camp as we were, and still are, a whole day behind our scheduled time to arrive in Settler Creek.' He cleared his throat.

'So, Miss Wyatt, this man Coleman must have found you and bargained with the Indians to set you free?'

Clay dismounted from the chestnut's back.

'Wasn't quite like that,' he said wryly.

A Mennonite emigrant cried out fervently as emigrants gathered around, 'Whatever it was like, praise the Lord, be joyful, Miss Wyatt's saved!'

'Amen,' agreed his wife as folks cheered.

'Well, Miss Wyatt, you obviously owe Coleman a debt,' Drury stated. His eyes roved over the new garments she wore. He vowed, 'I will see he is repaid, every last cent.'

'Did I hear the name Coleman?' A tall lean man with an unhealed deep scar running down his left cheek pushed his way through the emigrants. He had thinning hair, most of his shiny scalp like the shell of an egg. 'Clay Coleman?'

'That's me,' Clay said.

The tall man's dark eyes narrowed. 'Coleman who used to scout for the Fort Adobe bluecoats a few years ago?'

'I'm back on their payroll,' Clay told him.

'Congratulations,' was the mocking reply. 'My name's Lucas Henderson.'

'Figured so,' Clay said quietly. He addressed the emigrants, 'Some Comanche renegades led by Chief Red Claw have been causing big trouble.'

'Well, I've heard a few stories,' Henderson said, shrugging.

'More than just stories,' Clay corrected him. 'They've been supplied with rifles and Fort Adobe re-hired me to poke around.'

For a long moment Henderson's dark eyes remained fixed intently on Clay.

'Well, I'm the professional trail scout hired by this

52

outfit to guide them safely through to Settler Creek,' the scar-faced man drawled finally. 'Mr Drury's woman is beholden to you.' He conceded with a wan smile, 'You're welcome to stay with us tonight, just one night, Coleman, then you'll ride out. I'm sure you have other trails to ride for the army.'

Clay faced him squarely in the fire glow. He asked bluntly, 'Why did you make night camp here in Rattlesnake Pass?'

'It's none of your damn business, Coleman,' Henderson flared, his face suddenly reddening. 'But I'll tell you anyway.' He explained gruffly, 'Fact is, we've had company.'

'Twenty, maybe thirty Comanche riders stalking us,' Drury supplied.

'Keeping their distance, mind you,' one of the emigrants spoke up. 'Just shadowing us.'

'Looked like they were armed with rifles,' another westerner contributed.

'Just before sundown we gave them the slip but no doubt they're out on the plains somewhere,' Henderson said. He folded his arms. 'I made the strategic decision for us to sneak quietly into this pass to be completely out of their sight.' He reasoned, 'It was so we could light a fire and rest easy for the night.'

'But this is a real narrow pass,' Clay Coleman argued. 'If the Comanches decide to attack, you'll all be like rats in a trap.'

'You're a flaming scout, same as me,' Henderson snarled, 'and you know damn well Indians don't attack at night. It's against their religion.'

'I'm not sure Red Claw and his renegades are particularly religious,' Clay countered.

'I'm scout of this goddamn outfit,' Henderson declared again, glaring at him. 'I make the decisions. We shelter here tonight and because we've been followed by a big bunch of Indians who may possibly be hostile, then we'll break camp at first light, continue right down Rattlesnake Pass and take the old trail through the big mesa country.'

'Which is closer to Red Claw's territory,' Clay pointed out.

The emigrants exchanged concerned glances. They'd all been on edge since noon when they'd seen a line of mounted Comanche warriors first watching the wagon train, then riding the trail about an hour behind them. The Indians had vanished later in the day and an eerie silence then settled over the plains when Henderson led the wagons into the pass.

Now they felt uneasy.

'Listen, Coleman, drink our coffee, eat our grub, get some shuteye and then get the hell out of here,' Lucas Henderson dismissed him.

'If you take the big mesa trail, I'll be staying,' Clay said firmly as even more emigrants gathered around. He gave them his reason, 'You could need an extra gun.'

'Lucas!' A thick-set man with a bushy black beard pushed through the other emigrants and confronted Henderson, whose right hand was now hanging close to his holstered gun. He rebuked his emigrant trail scout, 'Keep your flaming shirt on.'

Henderson protested, 'Listen, Mr Grantham, I've been put in charge of this outfit -'

'But I'm the wagon-master, which means I'm trail boss,' Grantham stated. 'You've made the decision to spend the night here in the pass and that's where we'll stay. However, I won't rest easy knowing tomorrow we'll be taking our wagons closer to Comanche Territory. And, if we still do, that extra gun Coleman offered could come in real handy.'

Enraged, Henderson shook visibly, but nodding heads made it obvious that the emigrants were siding with their wagon-master. They were saying it openly now. Although Henderson had brought them this far, they'd been spooked by seeing those Comanche braves, they were divided on the wisdom of being here tonight in Rattlesnake Pass and a clear majority would sleep easier having Clay Coleman around. Moreover, some emigrants, in particular the Mennonites among them, had felt guilty at leaving Mr Drury's mail order bride so soon to her fate. They should have searched one more day, even two or three, many had argued. At least Clay had found Abigale Wyatt, rescued her and returned her to her fiancé.

They felt safer having him around.

'I'll decide in the morning,' Henderson announced, affirming bluntly he was still in charge. 'Meantime, everyone needs to eat and sleep.'

'I have a suggestion,' Clay spoke up.

Lucas Henderson fumed, 'And what the hell would that be?'

'We post two sentries,' Clay said.

'Not necessary,' Henderson shrugged off the suggestion.

Clay persisted, 'I'll be one of them.'

Henderson held back from belching expletives, instead gritting his teeth and ordering, 'Have it your way. You take the northern side of the camp.'

'Fine by me,' Clay agreed.

'And I'll take the southern side,' Drury spoke up.

'Are you sure you wouldn't prefer to spend tonight with

your rescued fiancée?' Henderson asked, somewhat sarcastically.

'I'm a man who knows where his duty lies, Mr Henderson,' Drury replied stiffly.

'Suit yourself,' Henderson said, lighting a cigar.

'Let's get back to supper,' Wagon-Master Grantham said.

The westerners dispersed, gathering around the cooking fire.

There were three families with children, all coming west to start a new life in a long valley just outside Settler Creek. Elias and Sally DuBois were a Mennonite couple, hoping to establish a church. Grantham, a former greycoat corporal in the Civil War, and his wife Amelia, were older than the others, well into their sixties. Widow Avis Whitely was on her own, just her and her large Conestoga wagon stacked with furniture ready for a new home. Seated together by the fire were Sol Brown and his three brothers, all seeking fame and fortune out west. Jason McKenzie and his Mexican wife, Maria, rode in the smallest wagon. There were whispers that McKenzie had once been a gunfighter in Colorado but no one dared to ask him. Besides, it was none of their business. Like them all, McKenzie was seeking a new start in life.

The ninth wagon was the smallest.

It was crammed with supplies, spare saddles, food, barrels of spare water and even two wooden coffins, although these were discreetly covered. The emigrants figured they were carried in case they were needed on the long trek west. While on the trail, Drury was in the driver's seat. Tomorrow Abigale would resume her place beside him. It would be a good opportunity to talk. The trail scout, Henderson, had provided this supply wagon, but there was no room to sleep in it. Henderson, Drury and Abigale mostly slept on the grass close to the glowing night fire. Drury in particular had complained about this. He'd tried unsuccessfully to persuade the Mennonite couple to let him put his bedroll in the rear of their wagon but Elias and Sally Dubois had politely declined. They might be well into their sixties but they still indulged in robust, noisy love-play at least twice a week, three times if Sally was in the mood, which was often, and they didn't want Mr Drury to be listening close by. However, they had agreed to transport his leather case containing fresh shirts, pants, underclothes, socks and boots together with his ornate boxes of Turkish cigars in their wagon.

Tonight the emigrants shared supper and coffee around the warm, ruddy glow of the fire.

Henderson seemed to have calmed down and he joined McKenzie and Sol Brown to play poker, with the cards being dealt on an old southern army blanket. Clay saw Drury and Abigale seated together with their backs to a wagon wheel. Drury was talking earnestly to her, almost like he was lecturing her, and he noticed that she stared straight ahead. However, more than once her eyes found Clay Coleman and lingered on him.

After supper, Clay figured it was time to take up his post.

He left the firelight and made his way between the McKenzie and DuBois wagons. He found two flat rocks by the shallow creek that meandered through Rattlesnake Pass. Placing his rifle on one, he sat on the other and kept watch on the timbered terrain to his north. Behind him, the cooking fire burned low and the emigrants mostly went to sleep in their bedrolls. He saw where Abigale was sleeping, alone, just touched by the dying glow of the fire.

He heard a sudden rustle in the long grass and the moonlight showed him a fat rattler slithering to the water's edge. He remembered this place was called Rattlesnake Pass because the earliest pioneers had encountered an unusual number of venomous snakes here.

Clay kept watching, his hand ready on his holstered Peacemaker but the sidewinder slipped away into the darkness.

However, the sound of this rattlesnake in the grass wasn't the only one that came to Clay Coleman as he kept his lonely vigil. An hour later he heard the crunch of boots coming from the far side of the creek. Maybe it was someone fetching water, although that would be unusual this time of night.

Still listening, Clay picked up his rifle.

The crunching stopped.

Clay rose to his feet and walked quietly to the creek.

He saw the snake again, coiled on a small rock. The rattler fled swiftly into the night and once again Clay heard the rustling sound above the murmur of the creek.

Clutching his rifle, he waded through the water and reached the other bank, where he halted and listened. That's when he heard more heavy footfalls from the timber. He could call out and challenge whoever it was had snuck out of the wagon camp, but he decided to trail the person instead.

Keeping his head low, moving slowly, he headed through some darkened sagebrush to the edge of the timber. Here he stopped and listened again, but this time he heard only a tawny owl hooting in the moonlight. He wove his way through a copse of ancient cottonwoods, passed a solitary towering arrowhead pine and came out on the other side of the timber.

Just ahead, the stark walls of Rattlesnake Pass crumbled over a flat, moon-drenched balcony ledge. It was a long slab of rock that overlooked the deep darkness that was Comanche Territory.

Clay had been here before.

The trail through the pass slewed across that ledge, then sloped down and meandered through an ancient canyon that Clay remembered was littered with craggy boulders. It was a deep walled-in valley that could easily conceal a hundred warriors, one of many potential hazards the emigrants might have to face if their wagons took this trail.

Clay was about to leave the timber and keep searching when he saw the dark, lean outline of the man he'd been following. He'd just emerged from the shadows, walking slowly across the granite ledge.

Watching closely, Clay saw another furtive movement.

Three riders had just mounted the ridge and now waited for the man on foot to reach them.

Even from this distance, Clay made out the riders to be Indians.

Keeping to the shadows of the western wall of the pass, Clay left the timber and ran to the very edge of the big balcony ridge. Here he could hear their low voices on the wind.

He eased closer and crouched in a crop of smooth boulders that lay halfway across the ledge like old discarded marbles.

Now he could see the three riders plainly.

They were definitely Indians, all carrying rifles.

Snatches of Indian talk drifted to him, confirming the three riders were Comanches. Then he heard the man on foot speak and Clay recognized the rasping voice of Lucas Henderson.

He knew this was no chance meeting. At this time and in this remote place it had to have been prearranged. Clay considered these three Indian riders might well be part of a larger bunch, maybe not far away.

One of the Comanche bucks raised his rifle to the stars and another whooped triumphantly while the oldest warrior, who had long grey hair, continued to converse earnestly with the wagon train scout. Henderson raised his right hand and pointed north-west, the direction where the trail ran along the edge of Comanche Territory. Finally, the grey-haired rider said some words to Henderson but they didn't carry on the wind. When he'd finished speaking, the oldest warrior raised his right hand to signify the meeting was over and turned his pinto pony's head.

Henderson said something to each Comanche rider, then stood watching as they rode in a line to where the down trail sloped to the canyon below.

Clay crouched low behind the boulder as Henderson came towards him, his boots scraping the granite rock. Momentarily, Henderson's body blocked the moonlight as he reached the boulder, then he shuffled past. Clay glanced back at the Comanche riders. He could still just see them, dark shadows under the stars. He waited until finally they took the old wagon trail and disappeared from view, then he stood up.

Henderson was already some fifty paces away, marching back to Rattlesnake Pass.

Clay's words cut the silence like a knife.

'So what was that pow wow all about, Henderson?'

The scar-faced trail scout halted, his boots frozen to the rock.

'None of your goddamn business, Coleman,' Lucas Henderson grated without turning his head.

'You having a friendly midnight meeting with Comanche Indians means I'm making it my business,' Clay Coleman said slowly. 'What the hell's going on, Henderson?'

'It's not what it looks like,' Henderson said slowly, playing for time as his right hand edged inch by inch towards the Colt .45 nestling in his leather holster. 'Nothing wrong with negotiating a safe passage for the emigrants with some of my Comanche warrior friends.' His long spidery fingers stroked the pearly grip of his gun. 'After all, it's the sort of thing a good trail scout does – wouldn't you agree, Coleman?'

'Turn around, face me, then we'll talk, Henderson,' Clay demanded.

'Sure, Coleman, sure,' Henderson said softly, fingers touching, clutching, then lifting his gun.

Henderson turned slowly but Clay saw the moonlight's glint on his Colt .45.

Two guns seemed to thunder in deadly unison.

However, Clay's rifle bullet blasted high into Henderson's chest a split moment before the Colt was fired and the scar-faced trail scout lurched sideways, slamming hard into the trunk of a lone pine. There Henderson slithered to the ground, his gun still pumping bullets that ripped past Clay and screamed into the night.

Finally, Henderson's head fell to one side, his fingers lost their grip on the Colt .45 and it dropped to the pine needles.

The gunfire echoes faded into the silence of the night but it was a silence suddenly shattered by the drum of horse hoofs.

Turning sharply, Clay saw the three Indians back on the ledge.

Hearing the gunfire, they'd returned to find out what was happening and were coming his way. Clay lifted his rifle again and shot the foremost Comanche rider clean out of his cloth saddle. The Indian lay sprawled in a patch of grass but the other two kept charging towards Clay.

The army scout raised his rifle.

A bullet whined past Clay's left ear as he pulled his trigger and emptied another Indian saddle. His fellow braves dead, the oldest Comanche dropped flat to his pony's back as Clay's next bullet screamed inches from his scalp.

The warrior turned his mount and with his long grey hair streaming behind his head, he rode furiously in retreat back over the ledge. Clay lowered his rifle as the fleeing Indian reached the top of the trail and fled.

That's when Clay heard the sound of voices and drumming boots.

The men from the wagon camp were surging down the pass towards him.

CHAPTER FIVE

First light saw the westbound settlers gathering around the blackened remains of last night's cooking fire. Most of the emigrants had spent a sleepless night. Their hired scout, Lucas Henderson, had been hastily buried a few minutes after midnight while Elias DuBois read some quick, pious words from his Mennonite Church prayer book. After the brief ceremony, a boulder was rolled over his grave so the coyotes couldn't dig him up. By the time the burying had been done, the two dead Indians on the ledge had been quietly collected too and taken away by unseen riders, which confirmed Clay's suspicions. The three who'd met with Henderson had been part of a larger bunch waiting somewhere just beyond the pass, probably down near the trail the emigrants were to take.

And he didn't think those Indians had friendly trading on their minds.

Now, as the sun showed over the eastern rim of Rattlesnake Pass, Wagon-Master Grantham, coffee mug half full of steaming brew, spoke earnestly to the worried emigrants assembled ready for today's trail.

'I like to think the best of folks, specially a man I hired personally, but we have to face facts,' Grantham told them ruefully. The emigrants listened in silence, broken only by the crackle of wood in the dying cooking fire. 'Henderson went against what most of us wanted. He made us camp last night in this pass. He wasn't even going to post sentries but Coleman here warned us of the dangers and so we posted them.' Some of the men nodded their heads. A couple murmured their thanks to Clay, who'd joined the early morning meeting. The wagon boss continued, 'Then Henderson snuck out. He didn't tell anyone. What the hell would he go on a midnight walk for? The good of his health? Well, it was to meet up with some Comanche riders under cover of dark.' Grantham raised his voice as he said grimly, 'I'll leave it to every man and woman here to decide what Henderson's motive was.'

'I think it's obvious, Mr Grantham,' Thomas Drury spoke up, answering for most of them.

The settlers voiced their agreement.

'I'm grateful to Clay Coleman,' Grantham declared. 'If he hadn't followed Henderson and seen him talking to the Comanches, they might well have attacked us right here in the pass, or tomorrow in one of those canyons Henderson was planning to take us through, murdered the men and taken our women—' He lowered his voice, reminding them all soberly, 'Like they took Miss Wyatt.' Abigale, standing apart from Drury, looked at her feet. No one saw the tears in her eyes as Grantham continued, 'Now I know Coleman is working for the army right now, but I'm hoping, in fact, on your behalf, I'm asking him if he can spare a couple of days from his duties to be our trail scout and guide us safely to Settler Creek.' He turned to Clay, who stood drinking his coffee alongside the Mennonite couple. He called out, 'What do you say, Clay Coleman?'

Clay let his eyes rove over the assembled emigrants.

They were scared, bewildered by Lucas Henderson's betrayal of them. Most of them had seen Comanche warriors apparently stalking the wagons yesterday and many had noticed the rifles they were armed with. They were still two, maybe three days out from Settler Creek and one young mother, sobbing softly as she contemplated the risks ahead, clutched both her children to her skirts. There were others too with nervous looks on their faces. Even Jason McKenzie seemed concerned. He might have been a former hired gunslinger, but he'd probably never faced hostile Indians.

The emigrants waited upon the army scout's reply, hoping and trusting as the Mennonite couple prayed out loud.

Abigale raised her eyes and she too looked straight at him.

'I'll ride along with you,' Clay agreed.

As they cheered and Abigale clapped, Grantham said, 'Now I feel safer.'

'Me too,' Drury admitted.

'Praise the Lord!' the Mennonite couple said in triumphant unison.

Clay addressed the emigrants, 'Hitch your horses to the wagons. We'll move out in ten minutes, back on to the plains trail most westerners use. We'll stay on that trail because it leads through mostly open country. I'm not sure whether we'll run into trouble or not but as a precaution, the womenfolk can be wagon drivers while the men ride either side. I'll ride up front.' Their new scout concluded, 'Everyone, men and women, keep your guns loaded and ready to use. That means rifles, six-guns, shotguns, the lot.'

'You heard Scout Coleman,' Wagon-Master Grantham hollered out. 'Get ready to roll the wagons!'

With Clay Coleman leading, the wagons left their night camp, headed back through Rattlesnake Pass and then returned to the open trail they were originally on. Dark cloud banks clung to the southern rims and a brisk early morning wind sweeping across the plains made their wagon canvas flap as the emigrants set their faces westward.

The Grantham wagon was the first in line, with the wagon-master's wife Amelia perched on the driver's seat. She had two double-barrelled shotguns resting together over her ample lap. Close behind came Widow Avis Whitely in her cumbersome Conestoga. Even the widow had a pistol tucked under her belt and an old hunting rifle, albeit a trifle rusty, close by at her feet. She was followed by the Mennonite wagon, then the rest in line. Lumbering behind the others was the supply wagon driven by Abigale. She held a rifle handed to her by one of Sol Brown's brothers. Like the other men, her Mr Drury was riding alongside the wagons. He held a rifle in readiness. Although Clay scouted just ahead of the wagons, every now and then he rode back down the wagon line to check all was well and Abigale made sure she flashed him a quick smile each time. And Clay Coleman noticed.

Now, mid-morning, Clay's experienced eyes ranged over the grassy plains ahead. He saw the distant Old Glory River they had to ford and the darkening rims that hung over the trail further on from the crossing. Looking back from time to time, he noticed two Comanche riders watching them. They were in the mouth of Rattlesnake Pass but as yet he saw no others, nor even a glimpse of smoke.

As he rode, Clay thought about the two white men he'd killed, Burgan from Broken Bow and now Henderson, long-time wagon trail scout. Both these men had tried first to kill him. But why? He'd never exchanged an angry word with Burgan and as for Henderson, if his midnight meeting with the Comanches had been a mere innocent rendezvous with friends, why hadn't he simply said so instead of drawing a gun?

Clay reached the eastern bank of Old Glory.

He knew this ford well because he'd scouted this way at least half a dozen times during his former time at Fort Adobe.

It was normally shallow and wide, but right now muddy water surged against its banks as the river was being fed by melting snow from the northern mountains that ringed distant Comanche Territory. From past experience, Clay knew water would be lapping stirrups soon after they entered the river, but when they reached the middle of Old Glory, their horses would be swimming and wagons floating. It would not be an easy crossing but the alternative was to head south into the red canyon country and head over the river at Cowpuncher's Ford, extending their journey an extra five days, maybe longer. Even then, the river could still be running high, maybe pounding its banks.

He decided the wagons would ford Old Glory here.

Clay waited until Abigale's wagon latched on to the line.

It certainly had been lagging behind the others and more than once he'd turned his chestnut back so he could ride alongside her.

With all the wagons waiting in a line, Clay nudged his horse into the water.

He rode through tall reeds, stood in his stirrups and motioned Amelia Grantham to follow.

Old Glory was certainly running deeper than he'd previously known. Murky water lapped his chestnut's knees, then rose swiftly to splash its chest and flank. Rusty snorted as Clay urged him further into the river. Behind Clay, Amelia Grantham flicked a whip over her horses, prodding both geldings to pull the wagon through the reeds. Her husband rode alongside, yelling at the horses. Then came the widow, Avis Whitely, standing tall as a willow, cracking her whip too.

Clay rode to the middle of Old Glory River and by now the current was so deep it flowed past his chestnut's shoulder and thigh. Now his horse was swimming and the river flowed over Clay's legs. He kept urging his horse on. Pushing ahead into more shallow water on the far side, he turned in the saddle. Amelia was doing fine, so was Widow Avis. Their horses were swimming, their wagons floating behind them as they came to the deepest part of the river.

However, Abigale, bringing up the rear, was having trouble, her wagon wheels sinking into black mud. Leaving Grantham to direct the emigrants, Clay rode the chestnut back, splashing across Old Glory. Unlooping his saddle lariat, he attached one end to the front of Abigale's wagon, the other to his saddle-horn. He positioned his chestnut alongside her horses and signalled her to use her whip. Together, his horse and hers pulled the wagon slowly out of the mud. The wheels began to turn, black mud flew and splattered the reed tops until the wagon lurched out of the shallows further into the river. By now half the wagons had reached the other bank, emerging from the river with water slewing from their sides and there they waited as Clay assisted Abigale to reach the middle of the river.

Suddenly Grantham's warning shout echoed over Old Glory.

The wagon-master was standing high in his stirrups, pointing at a low ridge that shadowed the trail ahead.

Half a dozen mounted Comanche braves were there, watching the emigrants down at the river crossing. But there were more than just the handful on the ridge. Clay saw another eight riders cresting a hillock on the other side of the trail and when he glanced over his shoulder, he glimpsed two warriors prodding their ponies through the waving reeds. One of these riders behind them raised his rifle and fired a bullet that ripped through the supply wagon's canvas. Responding quickly, Clay levelled his own rifle, pulled the trigger and saw the Indian crash into the reeds, where he threshed wildly before collapsing head-long into the water. The other Comanche hastily backed his pony back out of the river.

Still riding alongside the supply wagon's horses, Clay kept the rope taut. The other wagons had swayed in the current out here in the middle of the river but Abigale's refused to float. Instead, the supply wagon kept its wheels on the shale bed as water gushed over its sides. Slowly, ponderously, the wagon was heaved through Old Glory's depths until finally it reached the western bank, where Clay retrieved his rope.

He rode up to where Grantham, Sol Brown and Drury sat saddle keeping an eye on the Comanche braves. The mounted Indians remained like statues on the ridge and hillock, just watching the wagon train below them on the flat.

'We're in open country – thanks to you, Coleman,' Grantham spoke on behalf of the others. 'They can't sneak up on us.'

'All the same, we'll keep the way we have been,' Clay told them. He repeated, 'Women driving the wagons, we men riding alongside.'

'Shall I give the order to roll the wagons again?' Grantham asked.

'Before you do, I'm going to check inside that supply wagon,' Clay announced. 'It's our smallest wagon but as everyone can see, it's moving real slow. In fact, only just made it across the river.'

'Been like that ever since we left Silver City,' Drury recalled.

'I offered to help Henderson load it,' Sol Brown recalled, 'but he didn't take up my offer.'

'Grantham, come with me,' Clay called the wagon-master. He turned to the other two. 'Brown, Drury, ride the wagon line and tell every man and woman to hang tight and watch those Comanches.'

Clay and Grantham dismounted by Abigale's supply wagon.

Abigale held the reins steady while Clay climbed inside. He pushed aside the wooden feed box and stood up under the canvas bonnet while Grantham clambered up to join him. A large sheet of dirty canvas made a bow over whatever was stacked there. This canvas was secured with ropes tied around wooden pegs nailed to the floor. Clay lifted his Bowie knife from its leather sheath and slashed the ropes. Then he pulled the old canvas free to reveal three large barrels, two wooden coffins and a pile of old saddles.

Clay nudged one pine box with his right boot. It was so heavy he could hardly move it. He saw that the lid of the coffin had been nailed down. Crouching, he used his

Bowie to prise the lid open. Nails flew over the wagon floor as Clay lifted the coffin lid.

Stacked neatly inside were over two dozen latest Springfield rifles.

Grantham held his breath as he stared incredulously at the cache.

In fact, the wagon-master stood dumbfounded as Clay Coleman's knife forced open the other pine box and exposed even more rifles.

'This is what those Comanche renegades are after,' Clay said grimly, looking over Abigale's shoulder at the riders on the ridge. They were still motionless, like a line of vultures just watching the wagons by the river. 'In fact, I reckon when I came upon Henderson having a pow wow with those Indians, he was actually making arrangements to deliver these rifles.'

The wagon-master began swearing like a trooper. 'Goddamn, lousy bastards!' Realising Abigale was sitting there just a few paces away, he apologised. 'Sorry for the bad language, ma'am.'

'It's quite all right, Mr Grantham,' she reassured him. 'In fact, I feel the same way as you do. I could cuss myself!'

Clay glanced at the barrels. He added slowly, 'And maybe Henderson was aiming to supply them with more than just rifles.'

Grantham blinked. 'Huh? You don't mean—'

There were two water barrels wedged together right behind Abigale's seat but the three that had been concealed by canvas were double their size.

Again, using his knife, Clay prised open the first heavy cork stopper.

'Reckon you can smell it, same as me,' Clay said.

'Flaming whiskey!' Grantham exploded.

'Renegade Comanches, brand new rifles, rotgut whiskey – a dangerous mix,' Clay told the wagon-master.

'Hell yes!' Grantham agreed. 'It would have been easy for them to have cut off this wagon, because it was always the slowest.' He lowered his voice. 'It would have been even easier on one of those narrow canyon trails the other side of Rattlesnake Pass.'

Clay uncorked the second and third barrels. They too were full of whiskey. 'Fired up with this rotgut, they may have been tempted to attack the whole wagon train too.' He added, 'Maybe that was the plan.'

'And I'm damn sure that ornery, lowdown, stinking polecat, Henderson, would have left us to our fate and snuck away to drink rotgut with his Comanche pards!' Grantham exclaimed hoarsely.

'Help me roll these barrels out of the wagon,' Clay said.

Together they tossed one barrel out of Abigale's wagon.

'Running guns and whiskey to Indians is a risky business,' Grantham said as they rolled the second barrel out. 'The white skunks would want to be paid and well paid, too. So how do the Comanches pay them?' Frowning, he remarked, 'They'd hardly have heaps of cash in their camp.'

Clay stated, 'That's a question I aim to find the answer to.'

The trail scout and the wagon boss heaved the last of the three rotgut barrels out of the wagon. Clay emptied his Peacemaker, shooting two holes in each of the barrels before he reloaded. Whiskey spurted like fountains into the sunlight and the Comanche riders stirred on the ridges as the gunfire echoes reverberated over the plains.

'Now for the rifles,' Clay said. He calculated, 'Reckon there's enough for every man and woman to have two each. There's ammunition in the coffins so we'll load every last rifle.' He raised his voice now. 'Abigale, I've a chore for you.'

'Just name it, Clay,' she said eagerly.

'Walk up the wagon line, warn the women to keep watching like they're supposed to be doing now and tell the men to come here to fetch the guns.'

Abigale climbed down from the wagon to do his bidding.

The Comanche warriors were on the move.

They began riding down from the ridge and hillock.

Abigale's walk became a run, relaying Clay's orders to the emigrants.

First Drury and Brown, then the other men, headed their horses straight to the supply wagon, where Clay loaded and handed out the shiny new Springfield rifles.

The Indians were looming closer.

The Comanche who'd ridden off leaving his fellow brave dead in the reeds now plunged back into Old Glory River. Clay handed six rifles to Jason McKenzie, two for the supposed gunfighter, two for his senora and two more for Widow Avis Whitely. The Indian who was halfway across the river began firing his gun and bullets splintered into one of the coffins. McKenzie rested five of his rifles on the wagon seat, then cool as you please, took quick aim with his sixth rifle and blasted the whooping warrior clean out of his cloth saddle. Dead before he even hit the water, the hapless Comanche was dragged under by the relentless current.

Seeing the riderless pony rearing in the river, the other Indians hesitated.

Meanwhile, the emigrants were ready, armed to the teeth, responding to Clay's order to roll the wagons.

73

Flanked by the men, the wagon train surged forward. The Indians who'd come down from the ridge fired a couple of shots but the fusillade of flying lead from the pioneers whistled around them. One Comanche brave plunged to the grass, another stopped a bullet high in his shoulder and rode away clinging to his pony's neck. The emigrants riding on the other side of the wagons began blasting at the Indians who were milling at the timbered base of the hillock. Three Comanche riders fell, the others retreated into the trees. The men riding alongside the wagons all emptied both of their two rifles, then as they reached to reload, the womenfolk cut loose with their guns and a barrage of bullets boomed across the waving grass. Another Comanche rider toppled from his pony. Right alongside him, a young warrior clutched at his bloody shoulder. The women began shooting again.

That's when the Comanches vanished.

'Keep the wagons moving!' Clay yelled, riding back down the line.

'You heard the scout!' Grantham shouted, brandishing his two rifles.

Clay reached Abigale's wagon, much lighter now, rumbling along in a cloud of swirling dust. He took a quick look at their back trail. Just before they'd resumed the journey, he'd pushed the two empty coffins out of the supply wagon and they lay upended in the purple sagebrush. Two Indians were dismounting by the fast-emptying barrels of whiskey. Another Comanche was riding furiously to join them.

The wagon train rolled on, leaving the Indians and Old Glory River behind.

Noon saw the wagon train descend from the plains and wind its way across a long, wide valley. By mid-afternoon

74

the emigrant trail was back on the grassy flat. When it was sundown Clay ordered the wagons circled and even though they'd seen no more Indian sign since Old Glory River, he took the precaution of ordering four guards posted, all armed and ready just in case there was still trouble brewing.

Clay was one of the sentries himself.

The trail scout took up his post on the eastern side of the wagon circle, stationing himself under a towering arrowhead pine. He wouldn't sleep tonight. Instead, he would just watch and listen to the sounds of the night. He didn't mind being alone. It gave a man time to think and maybe figure things out. And right now he needed to do some thinking. When he'd originally worked as an Army Scout at Fort Adobe, relations with the Comanche tribes had been reasonably amicable. Sure, there had been some minor incidents between white settlers and Comanche braves but Clay had always managed to talk man-to-man with Chief Long Knife, and sometimes, if a northern tribe had been involved in some sort of trouble, with wily old Chief War Bonnet.

He'd smoked the peace pipe with both, each time as a welcome guest in their camps.

He'd never taken to Red Claw, however.

This chief, who was War Bonnet's half-brother, had been made leader of the Comanches who lived in the canyon country. He'd met him face-to-face but once, that time in War Bonnet's village. The meeting was to resolve a rancher's complaint that a couple of Red Claw's braves had rustled three steers. At the time, Red Claw had denied that his men had even been near the ranch, then concluded his tirade by contemptuously spitting into the ground by Clay's feet. Later, Clay hadn't been surprised to hear that Red Claw had turned renegade.

What white men in their right mind would even think about running rifles to the likes of Chief Red Claw?

They would have to be paid very big money – which brought him back to Grantham's question.

How in hell would Red Claw pay them?

That had been on his mind too.

A Comanche, even a chief like Red Claw, would hardly be in possession of a heap of ready cash!

However, some white men, and he suspected Henderson was one of them, were definitely running guns to Red Claw's renegades.

And Clay Coleman was going to stop them.

But even now he knew he needed help.

All being well, it would take all tomorrow and half of the following day to take these emigrants safely to Settler Creek, where he hoped to find Shoshone Sam, his old scouting partner. It would be good to catch up, even for old times' sake, and maybe, just maybe, enlist him to help. Whether he wanted to help or not, a man like Sam might have seen or heard something important.

He heard a soft footfall behind him.

Looking back over his shoulder, he saw a slim figure silhouetted against the rising moon.

'Clay,' Abigale called to him.

He was staked out on the ground, his back leaning against the tree trunk.

He stood up as she came closer.

'What are you doing outside the wagon circle?' he asked her. He reminded her sternly, 'Remember what happened before?'

'I – I just wanted to say something to you,' she replied falteringly.

He insisted, 'But shouldn't you be with your man?'

For a moment there was silence between them.

'Mr Drury is talking business with some of the other emigrant men,' Abigale again excused her presence here. 'Something about selling them calves from his father's spread so they can start their own herds once they fence their new land. It's all money-talk, Clay, and I formed a definite impression that I was in the way.'

Clay found himself thinking that an attractive woman like Abigale Wyatt would never be in his way but he kept that thought to himself.

'So your Mr Drury is a cattleman?'

She realized then that she hadn't said much about her fiancé to Clay. Of course, there hadn't been time for small talk. From the moment the trail scout had rescued her from that Comanche night camp, he'd been too intent on keeping them both safe. And, she told herself, she'd felt safe with him. Very safe.

'Mr Drury's father owns the Triple D ranch, just outside Settler Creek,' she said. 'Mr Drury told me all about it last night.' Abigale faltered for a moment. 'He also made it very plain his father was a very strict-living man, attends church at least once, sometimes twice, every Sunday.' She added quietly, 'After what's happened, I'm hoping he approves of me.'

'What happened wasn't your fault, Abigale,' Clay reminded her.

Abigale confided, 'Mr Drury agreed – that was, after a while.'

'So you told him?'

Abigale nodded. 'I think he knew anyway, Clay. He did mention however that many white women would have killed themselves rather than—' Tears flooded her eyes as she looked at her feet. Finally, she raised her eyes and looked straight at him in the moonlight. 'However, after much considering last night and most of today, Mr Drury made his big decision. He told me our marriage would still go ahead.'

Clay Coleman remarked wryly, 'I hope you don't have to call him Mr Drury all your life!'

'I understand from my fiancé that once I'm accepted into the family, then I can call him Thomas,' Abigale said.

Clay frowned. 'So you're on trial till then?'

'You could say that, Clay,' she said, resignedly.

'Well, you'll be fine,' Clay tried to reassure her, but he wasn't real sure.

Abigale told him, 'Mr Drury said I should become part of the family very soon after we get to the Triple D ranch. I'll have some duties, of course. I'll be expected to help his mother with the cooking, washing, cleaning and trimming their prize roses in the garden. She will teach me how to play the pedal organ because Mr Drury wants his woman to help entertain any guests they have over for dinner. Once there on the Triple D, I'll have my own room to sleep in, of course, but after the wedding, Mr Drury and I will live in another ranch house being built for us near the western fence of their land.' She remembered her fiancé's repetitious words. 'However, I'll still be expected to cook for the ranch hands, breakfast and supper every day.'

Clay raised his eyebrows.

He wondered whether this mail order bride had been told about her life out west before agreeing to come. There didn't seem to be any joyful anticipation in her tone. Rather, there seemed to be resignation.

However, she would be Mrs Abigale Drury and ultimately, when her husband's parents died, she'd have the prestige of being the wife of the man who owned the largest ranch west of Broken Bow.

Clay reminded her gently, 'You said you came out here because there was something on your mind, something you wanted to say to me.'

'Yes, that's right, Clay,' Abigale said softly. There was a tremor in her voice. 'It's difficult for us to be alone on the trail.' She hesitated. 'Some would say it's not proper anyway, since I'm Mr Drury's betrothed.' She hesitated and then said, 'However, I needed to be alone with you, even if just for a few minutes.'

'Well, we're alone now,' he said.

A sedge warbler bird whistled high in the big pine.

Abigale murmured, 'I needed to say thank you properly, Clay. You saved my life. I owe you. Whatever happens to me, I'll always remember that.'

He was about to say 'thanks weren't necessary' but in a sudden, bold move, Abigale took one step towards him, reached up and cupped his face in her hands. Standing on her toes, she pressed her soft lips to his right cheek. They lingered there for a long moment while she stood close to him, real close, touching him, then she stepped back.

Even in the moonlight he could see her flushed cheeks.

'Thank you, Clay Coleman,' she said earnestly.

Then Abigale fled back into the wagon circle.

CHAPTER SIX

They broke camp just as pallid pink showed and spread in the far east. With Clay riding ahead, they headed along the emigrant trail. Even though Clay only spotted a lone Comanche warrior watching from a distant rim, he still insisted on the men continuing to protect the wagons by riding either side of the rumbling line. The day passed without incident and by sundown they formed a wagon circle beside a meandering creek. The silent watcher on the rim had long vanished but Clay was still being cautious. Four sentries were posted and once again Clay maintained an all-night vigil under the stars.

Tonight no one came to keep him company and when Clay looked back inside the wagon circle he saw the mail order bride bringing coffee to her man. The memory of her quick kiss on his cheek and seeing her now in the firelight made Clay Coleman realize it had been a long time since he'd had a woman.

Too long.

He smoked a lonely cigarette.

Knowing they were on the last stretch of their westward journey, the pioneers rose early. As the camp sprang to new life, Clay took a quick walk through the blue gamma grass beyond the wagon circle, then forded the singing creek to take a look around. Satisfied there was no Indian sign, he snatched a quick meal of bacon and bread, drank coffee, spoke to the wagon-master and made ready to guide the emigrants along the last few miles to Settler Creek.

With the sun at their backs, they headed west and by mid-morning they glimpsed the distant town of Settler Creek.

Within minutes they passed two sprawling ranches to their north, the Big V and Reb Mortimer's diamond-shaped Lazy M. The wagons rolled by a disused mine shaft and three old deserted cabins, legacy of the very early days when a vein of copper had been discovered. The lode soon petered out and the next wave of westerners came to fence off slabs of land.

The trail swung south-west, heading towards the town limits. A large wooden sign with outstandingly bold green lettering told them they were now adjacent to the Triple D Ranch. The rich Drury spread rolled south from the wagon trail. Well-fenced, watered by a river gushing from the distant mountains, the grass was tall, waving in the breeze. Hundreds of longhorns grazed there, huge beef herds worth tens of thousands of dollars. Built prominently on a slow rise right in the centre of the land was an impressive stone ranch house. Smoke curled languidly from its two chimneys.

Thomas Drury left the wagon line and rode his horse to the gate.

Climbing down from the supply wagon she'd been riding on, Abigale walked to join her fiancé at the gate – and to admire the grassy empire that stretched for miles.

It was then Drury spoke briefly to Clay. Clearing his

throat, he said, 'I'm beholden to you, Coleman.'

Clay merely advised him, 'Look after her, Drury.'

The heir to the Triple D frowned. 'Of course, of course I will.'

'Clay,' Abigale spoke up, using his first name and causing a frown to crease Drury's forehead. She asked, 'What will you do?'

Clay replied, 'I'll catch up with my old trail scout friend, Shoshone Sam. Hopefully he still lives in Settler Creek.'

'Oh yes,' Abigale recalled. 'You did mention him that first night after you rescued me from those Comanches.' She said sincerely, 'I hope you find him.'

'So long, both of you,' Clay said to Drury and Abigale.

Abigale raised her right hand to wave but Clay was already riding down the wagon line ready to lead the westerners into Settler Creek. Now they were so close to town, the emigrant men climbed back onto their wagon seats and resumed driving alongside their wives. Sally DuBois mounted the light, almost-empty supply wagon. They were all in high spirits. It had been a dangerous, arduous trail, they'd escaped a deadly Comanche trap but they'd survived and a new life awaited them. Jubilation was taking over now. The Mennonite couple were singing hymns. Even McKenzie yelled out a loud 'amen' to their prayers.

The wagons rumbled past a sodbuster's cabin, crossing a long, sandy flat and followed the rutted trail downward towards the beckoning stone and log buildings of Settler Creek.

They came to a fork in the road.

The western trail led to Bitter Springs and the old abandoned military outpost, Fort Buffalo. It was thin, dusty and rarely used, just like it had been when Clay rode scout for monthly patrol.

The other trail headed straight for Settler Creek.

The town nestled below them, built on the eastern bank of a shallow creek that once it had left the town behind meandered past an old log barn that had been raised by Amos Brindle, the first ever pioneer to arrive here. Amos had long been laid to rest and when Clay had last passed through it was crumbling through disuse. Once past the barn, the creek joined Mormon River.

Clay kept riding and it took less than five more minutes for the emigrants to reach their destination.

Unlike Broken Bow, there was no 'welcome' sign but a thin, bearded rider, who'd obviously seen the line of billowing canvas approaching, was waiting for them. Clay hadn't been here for seven years so he probably wouldn't know many of the townsfolk, however, approaching the corral, he recalled this bearded man's face. He once worked in the Settler Creek Cattleman's Bank. Now he was ushering the dusty, creaking emigrant wagons into a vacant stock corral just a few paces from the first business building to greet them, a newly built undertaker's parlour.

The word of the wagon train's arrival was spreading.

A few of the emigrants had family waiting for them. Amelia Grantham was embraced by her son, who'd come west five years ago. Sol Brown was met by a vivacious young woman who embraced him enthusiastically. Some, like the Mennonite couple, Sally and Elias DuBois, alighted from their wagons and just stood looking at the town while Widow Avis Whitely was beside them, busy brushing the trail dust from her long dress.

Clay approached the bearded rider who'd taken the time and trouble to meet these new westerners. The welcomer was no longer a bank clerk. Rather, he introduced himself as Abel Gainsborough, the town mortician, who of course would be pleased to offer assistance to any folk who sadly might now or in the future need his services.

Then Gainsborough frowned and scratched his head. 'I think I know you! You've ridden this way before!'

'Name's Coleman, scouted for the cavalry, now I'm back,' Clay told him.

'It's all coming back to me,' the undertaker recalled. 'I worked in the bank here before I received my higher calling to assist the sadly bereaved. I remember you rode in here with some bluecoats from Fort Adobe.'

'More than once.'

'So where's Mr Henderson?' Gainsborough asked Clay, his grey eyes roving over the westerners unhitching horses from their wagons in the corral. 'We were expecting to see him lead this wagon train into town.'

'We buried him,' Clay said simply.

'What!'

'Saved you a chore.'

Gainsborough's face paled. 'Dear Lord! What on earth happened?'

'He stopped a bullet,' Clay told him.

The undertaker simply stared at him. 'A Comanche bullet?'

'No, mine,' Clay said bluntly.

'Some terrible accident, I suppose?' Gainsborough suggested, his face turning ashen.

'You could say he made one helluva mistake.'

The undertaker's jaw sagged. 'Oh.'

Clay demanded, 'Last I heard, Shoshone Sam, my old sidekick, lived in these parts. Where can I find him?'

Still shaken by the news of Henderson's untimely demise, Gainsborough struggled to give Clay a faltering answer. 'Sam and his squaw woman – they live right here in Settler Creek. Sam raised a cabin in Black Deuce Alley, it's right on the creek bank.'

Clay nudged Rusty, his chestnut, into a walk.

Leaving Gainsborough to wring his hands in bewilderment and some emigrants to say farewells to their trail companions to make ready for their new life, Clay rode out of the corral and entered the long, wide street that divided the town. The whitewashed sign simply called it Main Street.

Settler Creek had grown since he was last here. A school had been built, there was a new barber shop, three card houses and two churches, one Methodist, the other a Full Gospel Chapel, both opposite each other on Main Street. Tinny piano music floated over the town's main thoroughfare from the newly built Soiled Dove Saloon. There were two general stores. By far the biggest of these was Wolf's General Emporium, a new building erected right alongside the Soiled Dove Saloon. According to the scrawled words on two gaudy crimson boards nailed above their doors, they were both owned by 'Mister Wolf Lonegan'.

Clay only afforded them a quick glance as he rode on past, reaching the stone front of Adam Cohen's 'Gold, Watches and Jewellery' shop, another new business that had sprung up since he was last here. Across the street was the office of the 'Settler Creek Clarion'. Chalked on the blackboard out front was 'October 31st issue out today'.

The sheriff's office was on the next corner.

Boards had been nailed across the front door and its two cobwebbed windows shattered. Clay wondered what had happened to Sheriff Ravenscroft, who'd been lawman ever since the town's inception. He'd been a genial man, obese, waddling the street like a duck, but friendly and competent. Clay figured there was no law now in Settler Creek.

Riding further down Main Street, he reached the Black Deuce Saloon standing on the corner of the alley that bore its name.

The Black Deuce used to be the only saloon here, the oasis every man who rode in from a long trail made for, but it looked a mere shadow of its former glory. Unlike the Soiled Dove, which was almost bursting with sound, the Black Deuce was quiet as Boot Hill at midnight.

Clay remembered the Black Deuce well. When the cavalry patrol they led stopped off in town, he used to drink beer and play poker with Sam here by sputtering lamplight. They used to sit at the rickety table under an old wooden staircase.

He rode down the alley alongside the saloon, passed Doc Brock's repainted surgery room and headed by twin rows of old stone homes that had been built here in the very early days of Settler Creek.

The narrow alley ended where a log cabin sat precariously on the creek bank. According to Gainsborough's directions, this was Shoshone Sam's place, directly opposite the Preacher's House. Right alongside this cabin was a stone stable and a bay gelding tethered in the garden. Smoke was curling from the cabin's single tin chimney. Riding closer, Clay figured if the creek was running high, surging water would be almost lapping the cabin's back door. But, obviously, it had been spared any floods.

He dismounted, tied the chestnut to a solitary hitching post and walked towards the front door, which was pushed open even before he reached the porch.

Yes, his friend Sam was still with Kymana, the slightly built squaw he'd latched on to while wintering in a

Shoshone camp. She had long raven-black hair, now streaked with grey. Standing in the doorway, Kymana recognized her man's old friend immediately and she greeted him with a wide smile. The last time she'd smiled at him, she'd had six tobacco-stained teeth. Sadly, the number had been whittled down to two.

'Mr Coleman!' she exclaimed.

'It's Clay, Kymana,' he reminded her gently.

'Yes, yes, of course,' the Shoshone woman remembered what he'd insisted she call him the first time Sam introduced them. She blurted out, 'Welcome, Clay. Yes, welcome!' She was obviously astounded to see him, overwhelmed. It had, after all, been seven long years. 'Come in, please come in,' she invited without a moment's hesitation.

Ducking his head as he walked through the low doorway, Clay followed her into the parlour. It smelled of fried eggs and sour milk and dried mud. He remembered when Sam, like him, lived in Fort Adobe. Sam and his Shoshone squaw had been allotted a room there and he recalled it was never the cleanest and needed a scrub. Nothing had changed. Even Sam's ancient, rusty two-barrelled shotgun rested over two hooks on the parlour wall. When it came to Kymana, Sam had always told him in a whisper, 'She's not exactly the best cook or house-cleaner, but she sure makes up for it in other ways.' Then Sam would wink, chuckle and give him an elbow nudge.

'You like coffee, Clay?'

'I could use some,' he said.

She placed two coffee mugs that could do with a soapy wash and rinse on the table in front of him.

'Where's Sam?' Clay asked casually.

Kymana lifted the blackened kettle from the potbelly's hotplate.

She didn't reply for a while, simply pouring her strong brew into the two mugs. When this was done, she sat opposite him at the small, heat-blistered table.

She still remained silent, as if she was considering what to say, or whether she should say it at all.

'My Sam is in trouble,' she said after another long moment.

'What's wrong, Kymana?'

'Sam needs help, Clay,' the Indian woman said bluntly.

'Tell me about it.'

'My man has changed since you last saw him,' she admitted reluctantly. She added, 'But not for the better, Clay.'

'What do you mean?' he prodded.

'He leaves town and goes trapping so we can sell the pelts and eat meat. This is good. Good for him, good for us both. But when he's home here in Settler Creek, he spends time, a lot of time, in the Soiled Dove Saloon.'

'And he's there now?' Clay guessed.

The Shoshone woman nodded. 'Yes, he will be there now.'

Clay sipped his hot coffee, remembering his old saddle friend had been over fond of hard liquor and more than once he'd had to ration Shoshone Sam's whiskey out on the trail.

He decided, 'Then I'll go and fetch him home.'

She hesitated before blurting out, 'I'm not sure Sam would want me to tell you this, but there is someone he has to meet there the last day of every month.'

'And this is the last day of October,' Clay said quietly, recalling the Clarion's blackboard.

She told him, 'Sam has to wait in the Soiled Dove
Saloon until this man turns up. Could be any time. He's a
real filthy sidewinder! Unfortunately, Sam owes this snake
money, too much money. It's a gambling debt. He does
not have enough to pay him this month so – so there
could be, probably will be, trouble.'

Kymana let out a long sigh, finally relieved she'd
managed to spill it all out to Clay Coleman, a man she'd
always trusted and had missed for seven long years. Then
she said passionately and thankfully, 'It is so good you are
here, Clay.'

'Does this snake have a name?' he asked.

'They call him Slade.'

'The coffee can wait,' Clay said.

The Shoshone squaw warned, 'Please be careful, Clay.'

He strode outside and as Sam's woman watched from
the doorway, he headed on foot back up Black Deuce
Alley. He reached Main Street and made straight for the
Soiled Dove Saloon. Two old-timers were lounging on the
wooden boardwalk outside the saloon and there was a tall
man standing by the batwing doors. He was Abel
Gainsborough, the town undertaker, finished with wel-
coming the new emigrants in their covered wagons, now
here smoking a cigar. When Gainsborough saw Clay, he
headed inside immediately, letting the batwings swing to a
creaking standstill behind him.

Clay mounted the boardwalk and parted the batwings.

For a moment he stood there, his eyes taking in the
saloon.

At first there seemed to be nothing amiss.

The Soiled Dove smelled of redeye whiskey and cigarette smoke, which was to be expected. A long-haired
bartender was washing glasses behind the long wooden

bar counter that lined the far wall. Undertaker Gainsborough was talking earnestly with a man in a blue suit, starched white shirt and spotted necktie. Two men stood drinking and chatting to a couple of saloon girls, one quite young, in her teens, the other well past her prime. There was a poker game in progress. Strangely so, storekeeper Morgan from Broken Bow was there, hunched over his cards. He held them in his left hand, the other one still lifeless after all these years. Also in the game were two other men Clay knew. One was a stumpy former soldier, swarthy-faced Douglas Fisher, the other, Wesley Horn, a wiry old hairy-faced prospector who'd spent most of his life panning for gold without ever striking it rich. Both Fisher and Horn looked up, acknowledging Clay with a couple of nods as he stood by the batwings. After exchanging a few brief words, they returned to their poker game.

Close by, a pretty, buxom Mexican senorita in a colourful red and gold dress was playing the piano and another painted saloon girl, well in to her forties, was drinking alone, her whiskey bottle almost empty.

There was a man drinking alone too.

He was thick-set, completely bald, seated in the far corner of the saloon.

And Shoshone Sam lay crumpled on the floor in front of him. The former army scout had his face to the sawdust that covered the saloon floor. His corn-coloured hair was matted with blood still flowing down the back of his neck. The bald man had his left boot firmly planted in Sam's back, right on his spine, pinning him down.

Clay took three paces into the Soiled Dove.

The Mexican girl's fingers froze on the keys and the saloon was plunged into silence as the bald man, his eyes fixed on Clay Coleman, deliberately ground his boot into Sam's back, causing him to groan in agony.

'You Slade?' Clay demanded.

Shoshone Sam raised and then turned his head at the sound of Clay's voice. His face was battered, his cheeks bruised blue, blood seeped from his mouth.

The bald man stared at Clay with ice-flecked eyes.

'What's it to you?'

'Take your goddamn boot off my friend's back.'

'No one tells me what to do,' Slade said.

Clay reached him in moments and smashed a clenched fist into his gaping mouth. Slade fell backwards off his chair, spitting broken teeth and blood as he crunched into the bar counter.

Belching profanity, Slade clawed at his holstered Colt revolver but Clay's draw was much faster and the Peacemaker snarled first, pumping a bullet into the leg that had held Sam to the floor. Knocked off balance by the bullet's impact, Slade crashed over the saloon piano as the Mexican girl jumped from her seat and backed hastily away. Screaming in pain, Slade clutched the wound just above his knee and let his gun drop harmlessly to the floor.

Clay walked over to the fallen gun and kicked it towards Sam, who reached out and grabbed the spinning weapon. Stumbling, Slade lurched away from the piano and slumped into a chair, where he sat cursing, trying to stem the blood from his wound.

'Thank God you came,' Sam cried, climbing painstakingly to his feet. He smelled strongly of liquor, more so than the rest of this saloon. Once on his feet, he swayed. 'The bastard gun-whipped me. I thought he'd kill me.'

Still holding his gun, Clay stood over Slade.

'How much does he owe you?'

A third tooth slid from Slade's mouth and slithered in a stream of blood and saliva over his shirt.

'Fifty – fifty bucks,' Slade moaned.

'Thirty,' Sam corrected him.

'We'll call it forty,' Clay said. He reached into his shirt pocket, counted out the money from his Fort Adobe pay, and let it drop over Slade's boots. 'The debt's paid.'

Slade's bloody hand scraped up the money.

'I'll give you a piece of advice, Slade,' Clay said as Sam staggered towards him. 'Don't ever draw a gun on me again.' He warned, 'If you do, I'll kill you.'

Clay slid his Peacemaker back into its holster as Sam reached him.

He steadied his old scouting friend, watching carefully as the one-armed Buck Morgan went over to join undertaker Abel Gainsborough and the man in the blue suit.

It was the latter who rose slowly to his feet. He was tall, head and shoulders above most in this saloon, clean shaven with thin bloodless lips and a sallow complexion. With the Soiled Dove still steeped in silence, he adjusted his necktie as he addressed Clay. 'I'm Wolf Lonegan. I own the general store, I also own this saloon and I don't hold with gunplay on my premises.'

'But obviously you don't mind if a man who's had too much liquor gets beaten up here?' Clay demanded. 'You don't mind if ornery skunks like Slade get to bully folks?'

Lonegan said nothing for a moment. 'You're a smart talker, I'll give you that, Trail Scout Coleman.' His lips curled into a wan half smile. 'Yes, I know who you are. Buck Morgan's just told me all about you. You're a man on a mission, to unmask the sidewinders running guns to the

Comanches. Very commendable, all of us should be grateful. Yes, grateful, and I mean it. Thanks for coming here, Coleman.' Then Lonegan reached into his suit pocket and pulled out a shiny tin star, which he slowly and ceremoniously pinned to the front of his jacket. He coughed and then raised his voice. 'Not too many of you know this, but last night at a special town council meeting called and chaired by my esteemed community-minded undertaker friend, Mr Gainsborough, I was duly appointed sheriff of Settler Creek.'

He grinned as a wave of applause rippled over the Soiled Dove.

'Congratulations, Mr Lonegan,' the bartender called out from washing his glasses. 'We couldn't wish for a better man to lead us!'

'So, Coleman,' Wolf Lonegan resumed, 'I'm a man on a mission too, a very important one and that is to keep the peace in this town.'

Clay drawled, 'Well, I suggest you start with the likes of Slade.'

'I intend to start with a clean slate,' Sheriff Wolf Lonegan stated. 'I want Slade taken to Doc Brock's rooms to get patched up.' He beckoned to one of the card players. 'Fisher, that's a chore for you.' The one-time army trooper gathered in his winnings and ambled over to assist Slade, who was still groaning in pain.

The sheriff then told Clay, 'Coleman, I suggest you take your drink-sodden friend, Shoshone Sam, home to sober up.' He added, 'Because I'm in a good mood, I'm not laying charges against any of you. Now get out of here.'

Clay waited as Fisher hauled Slade to his feet and escorted him on to the street. With the batwings creaking to a standstill, Clay assisted the swaying, ex-scout outside.

Once on the boardwalk he heard Sheriff Lonegan's triumphant voice echoing from the saloon.

'Drinks on the house to celebrate my appointment.'

Walking right alongside Shoshone Sam, Clay crossed the street and turned into Black Deuce Alley. He could still hear the clapping, cheering and foot stamping coming from the Soiled Dove Saloon.

But he also heard his name called out.

Halting, he turned and saw the undertaker hastening towards him.

'Mr Coleman! Mr Coleman!'

'What is it?' Clay asked as Gainsborough reached him.

'A personal message from our new sheriff,' the mortician explained.

Still angry that a law officer had allowed Slade to bully Sam, Clay snapped, 'Save your breath—'

'It's good news I'm sure you'll appreciate hearing,' Gainsborough assured him, smiling broadly.

Clay relented, 'OK, let me have it. But don't waste my time.'

'Sheriff Lonegan has done some very quick thinking,' Abel Gainsborough said. 'He believes he may be able to assist you in your mission. He'd like a private meeting with you. Of course, he understands you've just finished a long trail and you'll need an early night's sleep so he'll open his general store tomorrow morning at eight o'clock. As it's the Sabbath Day, there will be very few shoppers, especially that early. You'll have plenty of time to talk in congenial surroundings.'

Clay kept walking with Sam. 'Tell Lonegan I'll be there.'

'I'll do that, Mr Coleman,' Gainsborough said, turning on his heels and retracing his footsteps to the Soiled Dove.

Clay led his stumbling old trail scout friend down the alley.

Together they reached the cabin.

Ten minutes later the process of sobering up Shoshone Sam began.

While Kymana reheated the coffee Clay had left on the table, Sam stripped to his long johns and staggered unaided to the creek. They heard him holler and utter some choice cuss words as he waded into the water. Fed by distant mountain snow, the creek water was cold enough to feel icy to Sam's bare limbs and torso. In fact, he yelped like a whipped dog as he waded in deeper, then ducked his head under the water.

Clay and the Shoshone squaw took their hot coffee and strolled around the back of the cabin to witness Sam splashing and floundering like a stricken fish. Sometimes a man on a mission needs a lighter moment and Clay's face wore a broad smile as he watched his old scouting partner shivering in the creek. Finally, puffing and blowing, Sam climbed the muddy bank, dressed inside the cabin and joined them for coffee.

By the time he drank three mugs of the Indian woman's strong black brew, Shoshone Sam, nursing a sore head, his hair still hanging wet like rat's tails, was close to being sober as a judge.

All the same, the Indian woman refilled his mug for the fourth time, just to make sure.

With sundown close, they sat around the parlour table.

'I owe you, Clay,' Sam said, rubbing his bruised face.

'You would have done the same for me.'

'Well, we certainly rode together – we would have done the same for each other,' Shoshone Sam agreed. He looked straight at his old scouting friend. 'I reckon this is no social call. Tell me more about why you're here in this neck of the woods.'

Clay spent five minutes filling in his old friend, starting with the message from Fort Adobe, the reason for his reinstatement as an army scout, his rescue of Abigale Wyatt and latching on to the emigrant wagon train. Sam whistled under his breath when Clay recalled the incident with Henderson and the discovery of brand new Springfield rifles being carried in the supply wagon.

'So you're here to find out who the hell's running rifles to Red Claw?' Sam reached for his tobacco pouch. 'It's the question quite a few folks are asking.'

Clay Coleman prompted, 'What are folks saying?'

'I've heard lots of crazy talk, like a Mexican outfit must be behind the gunrunning,' Sam told him. 'But how would they get the latest Springfield rifles to sell to the Comanche renegades? And, Clay, that's what Red Claw's bunch are, goddamn renegades. Most Comanches want to live in peace on their hunting grounds. In fact, two years ago I met up with Chief Long Knife for a trade. His people needed flour for winter, I swapped some bags of flour for skins. He was still real friendly, like he always was. But Red Claw has a killer streak in him. He's bad to the bone. I've always said that.'

Sam slurped down his coffee. 'But getting back to who's behind selling guns to the Comanche renegades, well, I don't believe the notion that it must be greasers from south of the border. I reckon the gunrunners are much closer to home. Makes more sense to me.'

Clay said, 'Figured if I came here you'd tell me if you have seen or heard anything.'

'And to sign me up to help you find the varmints?'

'If that's on your mind.'

'It sure is right now.'

'So apart from crazy talk about Mexicans, what have you heard – or seen?'

Sam leaned over the table and said earnestly. 'First I'll tell you what I heard. When I did that trade with my old friend Chief Long Knife a couple of years back, he spoke quietly to me. Real quiet in fact, so even his own family couldn't hear. He warned me that there was Comanche talk about Red Claw getting his hands on rifles. The word was white men, not just one but a whole outfit of gunrunners, would be supplying them. He heard no names mentioned, no details, just that Red Claw was boasting he would soon be the most powerful Comanche chief in the territory thanks to his big bunch of new pale-face friends.'

'Red Claw bad medicine,' Kymana joined in.

'Now I'll tell you what I saw,' Sam said. 'I was trapping just this side of the Muskrat River. It was in what the Indians call Cold Wind Canyon, on account of the freezing winds blowing down from the mountains. I'd just packed my pelts meaning to ride home when I saw two wagons on the other side of the river. They were headed north, towards Red Claw's territory. Now I figured that if they were emigrants, they must be crazy, so I started to ford the river to warn them. That's when they started shooting. Lead flying everywhere! One bullet nicked my right shoulder. Others whined past my head so I rode hell-for-leather back to the western bank. After they'd gone, I rode back over the Muskrat and checked the trail. It showed a helluva lot of wagon wheel tracks. Now I couldn't figure out why emigrants would just open fire on a lone rider, unless their wagons were carrying things they didn't want me to see. Later, when others began talking about guns being run to Red Claw, I remembered those wagons. In fact, I thought about them a lot.'

Clay built a cigarette. 'You'll have a sore head when you wake up tomorrow, Sam, but if then you still have a mind to join me, could you take me to that Muskrat River ford?'

'You know the answer, Clay.'

'I'm obliged, Sam.'

'I'm the one who's obliged!' Sam exclaimed. 'Hell, Clay, you saved my life twice when we both rode for Fort Adobe, once by Arrow Creek when you shot that deserter who was about to kill me so he could steal my hoss, then in Boulder Canyon where those crazy renegade half-breeds had me holed up. I'd have been scalped if not for you. Again, you helped me out today in the Soiled Dove.' Sam stated firmly, 'I owe you, Clay Coleman and if you want me, we're gonna ride together, just like old times.'

They shook hands across the table.

CHAPTER SEVEN

It was the hour after sundown and the town was still quiet, almost peaceful. Later, when bunches of cowboys rode in from the nearby ranches to spend their paydirt, raucous laughter and loud syncopated music from the saloons would ring out over the streets, alleys and homes. Clay and Sam sat either side of the parlour table talking about the best trail from Settler Creek to Muskrat River while Kymana, now with her apron on, stood over the wood stove cooking hash for all three of them. It smelled good to Clay. The hash was almost ready to be dished out when there was a soft, tentative knock on the cabin door.

Kymana took a quick peek between the window curtains, left her cooking pan, opened the door and stepped back.

'I'm Abigale Wyatt! Is this Mr Shoshone Sam's place?'

'Yes, this is Sam's home,' Kymana said, appraising the attractive young woman on her doorstep.

There was urgent desperation in Abigale's voice. She asked hoarsely, 'I don't suppose Mr Clay Coleman's here?'

'I sure am, Abigale,' Clay responded, taking three paces to join Kymana in the open doorway.

Abigale stood there, pale and lonely, clutching the

leather travelling case she'd brought all the way from Pennsylvania. Her eyes were wet, tears dribbling in little streams down her cheeks. When she'd left the wagon train in company with Thomas Drury, she'd still been wearing the same blouse and buckskin pants Clay bought for her, but now these clothes were streaked with dust.

Now she made a sad, tragic figure, tremblingly silhouetted against the rising moon over Settler Creek.

'Welcome to our home,' Kymana said immediately. 'Clay here mentioned you when we talked over coffee earlier. He said there was a chance you might pay us a social call some day but I sure didn't expect you tonight.' Her eyes narrowed. 'And by the look of you, something's gone wrong.'

'Everything's gone wrong,' Abigale said miserably.

Kymana didn't hesitate a moment longer.

She invited warmly, 'Come right on in, Abigale.'

Clay took Abigale's case and they ushered her inside.

'Meet my good friends, Kymana and Sam,' Clay introduced them.

Astonished at seeing their surprise visitor, Sam rose to his feet. He hardly smelled of alcohol now and he actually looked reasonably presentable, apart from the obvious bruises. He offered her a little bow. 'Pleased to make your acquaintance, ma'am.'

'What happened?' Clay asked her.

'My marriage is off, Clay,' Abigale said flatly. Her tears glistened in the yellowy lamp glow. Breasts heaving, she announced, 'I won't be marrying Tom Drury.'

It was the first time Clay had heard her call him anything but 'Mister' Drury, and unlike before, there was no respect in her voice. In fact, her tone was as cold as winter's frost.

'Sam,' the Shoshone woman prompted, 'these two folks need to talk. You and me ought to take a walk. Come on—'

'No, please don't leave on my account,' Abigale said hastily. 'I don't mind Clay's friends hearing this.' She added tremblingly, 'In any case, the whole town will soon know. Tom Drury plans to make an announcement in church tomorrow that his engagement to me has been terminated. Yes, folks, that was his word. Terminated. There will be no wedding, not with me anyway, although I'm sure a certain widow he met on the wagon train won't waste any time in getting her greedy hands on him.'

She sobbed deeply. Clay reached for her. He wasn't the kind of man to take liberties when it came to women but right now holding her close seemed the right thing to do. So Clay drew her against his hard strength, keeping her there while she cradled her head on his shoulder.

Watching on, Shoshone Sam raised his bushy eyebrows and managed an approving grin while Kymana was wide-eyed.

'You don't have to say anything,' Clay said quietly.

'Yes, I need to say it,' Abigale told him in a whisper. 'Clay, it was a nightmare. A horrible nightmare! Tom introduced me to his family. Even then I thought his father, Augustus Drury, was judging me by the way he looked me up and down, like he would some milking cow he might or might not approve of. They sat me down, a negro servant brought in tea in a cup. A real fine, fancy cup. I drank alone while Tom and his parents spoke together in another room. I kind of knew what the subject would be. Then they all came back in to the parlour. Augustus Drury said his son had told him all about what he called 'the Comanche incident'. Oh yes, he was sympathetic towards me. He agreed I'd been through a

101

terrible ordeal and sang your praises, Clay, for rescuing me. Just for a moment I thought all would be well.'

She lifted her face from his shoulder and looked directly into his eyes. Her voice broke. 'However, because Tom had told him those bucks had – had their way with me, "taken my precious jewel", as he put it, then I was tainted. Yes, "tainted", Clay. That was his actual word. I'll never forget how Tom's mother nodded her agreement in a real solemn way. Augustus Drury then told me their son, Tom, had forgiven me.'

'Forgiven you!' Clay exclaimed, his anger rising.

'That's what he said,' Abigale confirmed. 'Tom had forgiven me. Tom was willing to go ahead with the marriage, but he, Augustus Drury, had overruled him. He had the family's name and reputation to think of. The story of my capture would get around. He said I might even have a "half-breed baby bastard baking in my oven". Those were his words, Clay. I didn't bother to tell him that by now I knew it wasn't so because, as far as he was concerned, I was damaged goods.'

'And Tom didn't stand up for you?' Clay asked gently.

'His father did all the talking,' Abigale said, looking straight up at him. 'Tom just stood there staring at his boots, saying nothing, not even a single word until his father had finished. When that happened, Augustus Drury gave Tom a prod. Tom still wouldn't look me in the face. He just coughed three times and simply announced, "Sorry, Abigale, there can be no wedding." Just those few words. After telling me that, Tom turned his back on me, marched away and closed the door.'

Kymana couldn't resist her outburst. 'You're better off without the yeller-livered skunk!'

'Hell yes,' Sam chimed in.

102

'I've left my job and lodgings, come hundreds of miles all the way from Pennsylvania, only to be jilted,' Abigale said bitterly. 'And I have no money. Because I lost the engagement ring – the Indians tore it off me but they blamed me for its loss – Tom's father said they owed me nothing.'

'So how did they expect you to survive?' Clay demanded.

'I was coming to that,' Abigale said. 'Augustus Drury took me to town in the back of a small wagon. He was so ashamed of being seen with me, he didn't even let me sit beside him. I was lumped in the back like a sack of horse feed. It was right on sundown. Once there on Main Street, he told me I was sure to get employment in the Soiled Dove Saloon. After all, he said, I was one.' She stepped back, but still kept her hands on Clay's shoulders. 'I was so angry, Clay, that he would think I'd actually work as a saloon girl.' She confessed, 'I'm afraid I – I lost my temper, slapped his pious face!'

'Good for you, Abigale,' Kymana said enthusiastically.

Abigale admitted, 'I said things I shouldn't never have said and called him a lousy, lowdown, stinking polecat -'

'Good description but I could have done better,' Clay said, hiding his grin. 'I learned some pretty choice words in the army!'

'Yeah, he could cuss like the best of them if he needed to,' Sam backed him up.

Abigale said, 'Augustus Drury left me there on the street, I didn't know what to do. I certainly wasn't going into that saloon, or any other saloon, but I did remember what you said to me. You were going to look up your old friend, Mr Shoshone Sam.'

'That's me,' Sam announced proudly.

103

'You said you hoped he still lived here in Settler Creek,' Abigale recalled his words. 'I prayed that was so. I walked down the street and saw an old-timer lounging on the boardwalk. He was smoking a pipe.'

'Be old Clem Gable, the whiskery ole varmint,' Sam supplied.

'I asked after you,' Abigale said to Sam. 'Varmint or not, he told me where you live and here I am.'

'Any friend of Clay Coleman's is our friend,' the Shoshone woman declared. 'Please, sit down. Eat with us. Stay with us.'

'I can't take advantage of your hospitality,' Abigale protested.

'Oh yes, you can,' Kymana told her in a firm tone of voice as she ladled out servings of hash on four plates. 'My man, Sam, intends to ride out with Clay and help him unmask these filthy, greedy gunrunners who are causing mayhem throughout the territory. That will mean I'll be here all alone for a few days. Reckon if you've a mind to, you can keep me company.'

'I'm very grateful,' Abigale said, overwhelmed by her offer. 'At least I can take time to figure out how I'm going to get back to Pennsylvania.'

'We'll have a talk about that when I get back,' Clay promised.

'Thank you, Clay,' Abigale said quietly. 'I'll wait here for you.'

'While Sam and me are away, take time to rest up,' Clay advised. 'You've been through hell and not just the Comanche hell. I'd say you've been dragged through another kind of hell on the Triple D.'

'Don't worry about the sleeping arrangements,' Kymana stated. 'The men can sleep in the stable tonight.'

'Yes, Sam and me have a lot of talking to do,' Clay agreed before his old friend could open his mouth to utter a mild protest. 'In fact, we'll be talking and planning for most of the night so we might as well do that in the stable where we won't disturb anyone's sleep. Right, Sam?'

'Uh, yeah, right,' Sam mumbled, preferring to have his Indian squaw curled beside him under the blanket.

'So it's agreed,' Kymana confirmed as they all began eating the hot hash.

It was three hours later, right on midnight, when Clay and Sam tethered their two horses to the hitching post and bedded down on the stable straw. They talked for less than half an hour, mostly about the Muskrat River trail, before Sam began snoring as loud as a wild pig.

Clay glanced over at the cabin.

Doubtless the womenfolk had done their talking too because by now there was no light filtering through the front window curtain.

The cabin was wreathed in stillness.

Clay lay awake for a while, mostly thinking about the Drury family.

A gutless man like Tom Drury didn't deserve a fine-looking woman like Abigale Wyatt.

Not at all.

Then Clay drifted into the sleep he'd need before the long trail to Muskrat River began soon after first light.

Clay fed and saddled his chestnut horse while Sam yawned, rubbed his red eyes, stretched his still-bruised and aching limbs and brushed strands of straw from his clothes. The two trail scouts had awakened to a cold Sunday morning with rain spots pocking the alley dust. The town of Settler Creek was silent. Many folks were still asleep. Kymana and Abigale were both up and dressed, frying bacon and eggs and brewing coffee for the men who were about to leave them.

After eating their breakfast hastily, Clay and Sam checked their firearms and made ready to ride. Shoshone Sam grabbed his squaw and planted wet, whiskery kisses all over her bronze face while Abigale came to stand beside Clay Coleman, who was about to put boot to stirrup.

'Did a lot of thinking last night,' Abigale said softly. 'I was real tired but couldn't sleep. Had too much on my mind. Kept turning it over and over.'

'I'm sure you did after what happened,' Clay agreed.

'Fact is, you were on my mind, Clay Coleman,' Abigale shared with him.

'You've been on my mind too,' he said. 'If you intend returning east, I'd see you safely to Silver City where you can catch a stage—'

Abigale interrupted, 'I decided that I don't want to return to Pennsylvania. There's no one back there for me. No family, no one. I want to stay here, settle down out west.' She added, 'Make a new life for myself, maybe with someone.'

'When I return, we'll have a talk about that new life,' Clay promised.

'Please ride safe, Clay Coleman,' Abigale whispered fervently, her hands linking behind his neck.

Unlike that night outside the wagon circle, Abigale didn't just press her lips to his cheek. Instead, she pulled his head down and locked her lips with his in a long, passionate kiss that said more than mere words.

Gasping at her own impetuousness, she stepped back from Clay as Sam left the Shoshone squaw and marched towards his bay horse.

The two men mounted and rode down Black Deuce Alley.

Turning at the corner saloon, they started north up Main Street.

Sheriff Lonegan was waiting for them, smoking a Long Jack cigarette on the boardwalk fronting his store, Wolf's General Emporium. Seeing their approach, Lonegan, now wearing the town's shiny tin star pinned to his blue check shirt, consulted his fob watch. It showed seven thirty. Frowning, he stood up from his padded chair and strode on to the street.

Clay and Sam rode past the saloon, right up to the emporium where they slowed, then halted their mounts.

'I suggested eight o'clock,' Lonegan reminded them.

'That's what the undertaker said,' Clay recalled with a shrug. 'I decided to leave when we did and figured if what you had to say was real important then you'd be ready and waiting when we reached your store.'

Irked at what he considered to be a response bordering on arrogance, Wolf Lonegan took the cigarette from his lips and flicked ash from its tip. He was about to say that as lawman of Settler Creek he deserved respect but he decided to let the moment pass. Instead, he actually smiled.

'I want to say on behalf of this town and the ranchers who have spreads close by that we appreciate what you're aiming to achieve. You know, this used to be peaceful country.' Wolf Lonegan raised his voice in the early Sunday morning silence, sounding like an evangelistic preacher holding a street meeting.

'There was a time when a decent white man could ride this territory knowing he could do so safely. Then that

107

murderous polecat Red Claw rose to become chief of a bunch of Comanche renegades. As if that wasn't enough, folks all over the frontier are saying some ornery, lowdown rattlers, and that description's too good for them, have by all accounts been selling rifles to those red devils. Bastards! I shouldn't say that on the Sabbath, but I'll say it again – bastards. Gentlemen, this town is right behind you as you seek to unmask those gunrunners.'

'Well, thanks.' Clay picked up his reins. 'Now we'll be on our way.'

'But wait,' Sheriff Lonegan instructed. He strutted towards them. 'I've decided to help you.'

Clay asked, 'How are you figuring to do that?'

'Maybe some free grub from your store?' Sam hinted.

'I can do better than that,' Lonegan said. Turning around, he bellowed out, 'Doug Fisher! Wes Horn! Come out here! Pronto!'

Wes Horn the prospector emerged first, stumbling. He was holding a rifle in one hand and a grubby grey Stetson in the other. He looked like he'd had six drinks too many last night and like Sam, had just sobered up. Then came Fisher, two Colt .45 guns holstered at his hip. Doug Fisher looked surly, just the way Clay remembered he was at Fort Adobe. However, Clay had to admit, he'd been a competent soldier, a crack shot, the kind of man you'd prefer to have on your side in a tight corner.

'I'm proud to say these men, who apparently know you, both work for me,' Wolf Lonegan said. 'So as Settler Creek's lawful sheriff and a good citizen, I'm releasing them from their emporium duties on full pay to ride with you and help bring those gunrunning varmints to justice.'

Clay didn't need to hear Sam's urgent muttering under his breath because he'd already made up his mind.

'Again, thanks for the offer, Lonegan, but we're not looking for company,' he replied. 'Four riders heading into Comanche Territory are more liable to be seen by Red Claw's renegades than just two men.'

'But we can watch your back, Coleman,' Fisher pointed out.

'And, if it comes to meeting up with any scalp-hungry Injuns, you'll need some extra guns,' Horn spoke up.

Clay stated, 'Sam and me are riding together, just the two of us.'

'Suit yourself,' Wolf Lonegan said, puffing furiously on his cigarette.

'So long,' Clay said, nudging the chestnut into a walk.

'I was just being civic-minded, that's all,' the town sheriff yelled at the top of his voice as they rode further along the street.

'Yeah, you'll regret not having us along,' Fisher called out.

Clay and Sam didn't even bother to look back.

Settler Creek was stirring back into life as the two riders reached the town limits and set their faces for the north-west trail to Muskrat River. First they circled Drury's Triple D ranch and from a distance Clay saw the family mount a black-roofed carriage ready to drive to town and attend church. Thomas Drury took the reins. In Clay's view, the man was a coward for not standing up to his parents. He'd just discarded a mighty fine woman. Clay bristled at Augustus Drury's callous suggestion that Abigale work in the Soiled Dove Saloon. This morning the Triple D owner and his upright family would hear a sermon but the sermon Clay wanted to deliver couldn't be preached in a church.

Riding side by side, they reached the north-west trail.

It was like the old days when they'd often scouted together ahead of a cavalry troop heading out from Fort Adobe.

Clay and Sam left the last ranch behind and headed into the wilderness. The trail twisted lazily across a sagebrush plain, rounded a high pecan-dotted mesa, slewed into a shallow canyon and began a slow descent to Muskrat River. They rested their horses at noon, letting them drink from a creek that gushed over some flat red rocks. As the afternoon shadows lengthened, they saw the distant river flowing like a giant snake through the valley below.

They were halfway down the slope when Clay saw the smoke.

It was rising in blue-grey puffs from a northern rim.

They slowed their mounts, then halted in some juniper trees.

The Comanche braves still sending up those signals were almost two miles away, high on a balcony rim.

Clay figured that if the Indians had seen them, they were too far away to be distinguished as white men. They would look like mere specks moving over the plains. However, the smoke signals were a grim reminder that they were on the very edge of Red Claw's territory. Once they reached the Muskrat River, they would be on Comanche land.

They prepared to resume their ride when they saw an answering signal, more smoke starting to puff into the fading sky. This signal rose from the crest of a hillock, much closer, south of the trail they rode.

Watching through the trees, Clay saw a lone Indian sending up the signal.

It was quite possible he'd seen the white men from his

elevated position.

They waited in the timber while the shadows deepened.

When it was close to sundown, the puffs of smoke became mere wisps.

Clay decided to resume riding and they headed between the austere grey walls of Cold Wind Canyon. Having hunted in these parts, Sam knew the canyon well. At times bleak winds swept down from the mountains and became trapped in the canyon, making a man's hands and feet feel like lumps of ice. Right now, however, there was little wind, just a ghostly stillness.

They'd hardly gone half a mile when Clay spoke a warning.

'Watch our back trail.'

Shoshone Sam jerked his head around. 'Huh?'

'The mesquite flat.'

'Can't see anyone. It's almost dark anyway.'

Clay said softly, 'By the creek.'

Sundown's last golden flecks in one deeper creek pool provided just a glimmer of light behind them.

'No one's there—' Then Sam swore under his breath as he saw movement. 'Hell, yes! Damn pheasants running through the grass! One's flying!'

Clay said, 'They've been spooked.'

Sam looked around. 'Riders? Comanche bucks?'

'Not sure but we're not staying here to find out,' Clay decided. 'We're right here in the open so we'll ride quietly for cover.'

'Where?'

'Under that broken ledge,' Clay said. He added, 'Have your rifle ready.'

Clay had taken command, just like he used to when

111

they were both Fort Adobe scouts. Sam rarely argued with Clay because he was usually right anyway. Clay Coleman had an eagle eye and an uncanny sense, some would say, a sixth sense, when he rode through hostile country.

Now Clay led the way through tall grass to the crumbling ledge just east of the track they'd been riding on. They nudged their horses into the deepening shadows there and sat saddle waiting, watching their back trail. The country was steeped in silence now, a peaceful few moments before sundown.

Suddenly they heard the muffled thud of hoofs and the swishing sound of horses coming through long grass.

Two riders, cloaked by the dusk, drew adjacent to where Clay and Sam sat motionless in their saddles. They were Comanche warriors, one tall and lean, the other much older and stumpy, both now only moving at snail's pace in the gathering dusk.

'Reckon they're finding it hard to read our trail,' Clay murmured.

Sam lifted his rifle. 'There's just two of them. One each!'

'Wait,' Clay restrained him. 'Look back at the creek.'

'Holy Moses! Half a dozen more! We can't take on that many.'

'Don't intend to try unless we have to,' Clay said. 'Even if we took every last one of them, the gunfire would ring out all over Comanche Territory and bring all of Red Claw's bucks down on our necks.'

'So?'

'We wait till it's completely dark and sneak past them in the night,' Clay told him. 'Right now we just sit saddle and watch.'

'Here they come,' Sam warned.

Six Comanche riders splashed across the creek and headed straight for their scouts who'd ridden on ahead. Clay and Sam held their horses motionless. Sam's nervous bay gelding snorted a protest but the sound was lost on the slight wind blowing up from the river. Sam soothed his gelding as the half-dozen Comanche braves joined the other two.

'They're having a pow wow,' Sam said.

'More like an argument,' Clay amended, as some Comanche words drifted their way. 'It's dark. They can't read our tracks anymore. Some want to make camp, fry some meat and drink rotgut whiskey. They're saying they'll catch us in the morning anyway. Others sound more inclined to look around.'

'As long as the varmints don't look around here,' Sam muttered, ready with his rifle.

'They're settling for a night camp,' Clay observed.

Sam breathed a sigh of relief. 'So what do we do?'

'We wait till they light their fire then slip quietly down to the river.'

It didn't take the Indians long to have their cooking fire burning. The snatches of talk that came to Clay on the now-rising wind confirmed these were some of Red Claw's renegades. Apart from the squat one who sat alone with his firewater, the others were much younger, mostly arguing about who would lift the scalps of the 'white eyes' they were pursuing. Come daylight, they told each other, they'd pick up the paleface tracks again and hunt them down. Despite their arrogant boasting, when the older warrior spoke, they fell silent and gathered around. He had a soft voice, so Clay couldn't hear his advice, but it soon became evident.

One of the braves, the tallest, left the camp and headed

towards the river.

'He's been told to keep watch,' Clay said. 'We'll need to take care of him.'

They rode silently from under the ledge, shadows in the darkness.

Keeping their distance from the Comanche night camp, they circled past a nest of rattlesnakes stirring and slithering in the darkness and headed for the ford. The Muskrat River was mostly deep but Sam knew this one place where there was a shallow sand bar stretching from one bank to the other. They rode slowly now, circling bald boulders, crossing a thin creek, one of many that fed the Muskrat.

They were close to the river bank.

It was then Clay saw where the lone Comanche sentry had been placed. He was right by the ford, a lean shadow against the moonlit water.

Clay motioned to Sam to remain in the saddle and hold the chestnut's reins while he slowly dismounted and eased his way noiselessly through some sagebrush. The tall warrior was less than ten paces from him now and Clay could smell the whiskey he had taken from the night camp.

A tawny owl hooted in a nearby pine as Clay came closer.

Hearing a soft footstep in the pine needles, the Indian turned suddenly.

In a split moment Clay smashed his rifle hard into the Comanche's forehead. The tall brave buckled at the knees, toppling forward. Clay grabbed him, breaking his fall, then lowered his unconscious body to black earth between the pine's protruding roots.

He signalled Sam to ride to him.

There, on the river bank, Clay eased himself back into the saddle.

The rising moon shimmered on the Muskrat River but the towering arrowhead pine cast a long, darkening shadow over at least half the ford.

'That's where we'll cross,' Clay pointed to the shadow.

The scouts took a last look at the Comanche camp. The Indians were still standing around their cooking fire.

Clay and Sam rode past the motionless warrior into the Muskrat River.

Silent as ghosts, they rode through the darkness to the middle. Fast-flowing water lashed their stirrups as they kept to the submerged sand bar. Now, halfway across the Muskrat, they had to leave the big arrowhead's shadow and edge slowly into the moonlight.

A tree that had fallen into the river upstream speared swiftly past them, causing Sam's white-eyed bay gelding to suddenly let out a loud whinny.

The sharp sound carried back to the eastern bank.

Clay took a quick look over his shoulder.

The gelding's whinny had been heard.

Shouts of fury rose from the Comanche camp and within seconds the braves were running for their ponies.

'Ride like hell,' Clay said tersely.

CHAPTER EIGHT

The two scouts rode hard for the western bank, their horses threshing water into moon-flecked foam. Three shots rang out from the Comanche camp, every bullet winging wide into the night as the riders reached the shallows. Clay's chestnut blazed a path through the reeds, sending a disturbed beaver swimming frantically for its lodge. Behind him, Sam turned in the saddle and sent a shot whistling back over the river, then urged his bay gelding onwards.

Rusty mounted the western bank with water sheeting from its flanks.

Even though the moon and stars provided the only light, Clay could make out the trail Sam had told him about.

For a wilderness trail, it was wide, and well-used.

A bullet whined across the river and ripped splinters from a cottonwood trunk. Another was closer, ricocheting from a mossy boulder.

Clay urged his horse down into a hollow, Sam right behind him.

They heard thudding hoofs on the far side of the river,

then angry cries as the warriors came across the unconscious Comanche sprawled under the big pine. Moments
later they rode their ponies into the river.

The two scouts waited until they came out of the pine's
shadow into the moonlight, then aimed their rifles and
squeezed triggers.

The Comanche rider who was out in front of the others
caught Clay's bullet full in the chest. The buck toppled
into the river as his pony reared in terror. Sam's slug found
flesh too, boring into the shoulder of the next rider, who
slumped forward, clinging desperately to his mount's
mane. Clay fired again – and again, wounding another
Comanche. Unable to even glimpse the men shooting at
them from the darkness over the river, the Indians fired
haphazardly, spraying lead all over the western bank. Just
one bullet came close to the hollow, slicing through a thin
tree branch, sending it spinning away into the night.

Clay and Sam fired a second barrage, forcing the
Comanche riders to falter. Their war whoops died on the
wind.

One brave turned his pony around, then another followed. Two shots from Shoshone Sam decided them and
they fled back to the eastern bank.

Clay and his companion dismounted and returned on
foot to the trail.

'Light a match,' Clay said, crouching.

Squatting beside Clay, Sam obliged and the sudden
flare showed them a trail scarred by wagon wheel ruts.
Some were old, others were fresh, probably just made. So
intent was Sam in taking a very close look that he forgot
the match.

The flame burned his fingers. Yelping, he tossed the
match away and lit another.

'This is no emigrant trail because it leads right into Comanche Territory,' Clay agreed with Sam's earlier assessment. 'Your hunch is right. This must be the trail the gunrunners use to supply Red Claw's renegades with their rifles.'

'And by the looks of those fresh tracks, Red Claw's just received a new consignment,' Sam said grimly. This time he pinched out the flame before it scorched his already blistering fingers. 'So what's our next move?'

'You've taken me to this trail, like you said you would, Sam,' Clay said. 'I intend to follow the trail into Red Claw's country and take a look around. Now, if you want to turn back, no hard feelings. You could ride south down this side of the river, right out of Indian country. Reckon you could cross the ford by that abandoned outpost, old Fort Buffalo, then take the prairie trail and head home safely to Settler Creek.'

Just then they heard the ghostly hooting of a night owl from the other side of the river. Only both of them knew this owl was human.

'You know damn well what my answer is,' Sam stated. 'We ride together.'

As another owl hoot sounded, Clay said quietly, 'Then we ride now and put distance between us and those renegades.'

They headed back to their horses.

The moon rose full in the night sky and a thousand stars blinked overhead as they rode the wagon trail deeper into Comanche Territory. The trail clung to the river, rising slowly towards the snow-capped mountain range ahead. They rode past midnight into the early hours of next morning, resting their horses twice before resuming their trek.

Soon the Muskrat River was narrower, fast-moving, booming between two high banks.

The two riders circled a small Comanche camp, just six lodges around a near-dead cooking fire. An hour later they came upon another collection of lodges making a line along the Muskrat's bank. Probably a peaceful fishing village, Clay figured. Not every Comanche had joined Red Claw. All the same, they weren't going to risk being seen so they gave the camp a wide berth.

First light saw Clay and Sam in the shadow of the mountains.

Fed by melting snows and a dozen bulging creeks, the river raced even faster between its banks.

Clay kept a sharp eye both on their back trail and the other side of the river, but he saw none of the Comanche warriors they'd encountered last night. However, both the trail scouts knew from many years of experience in hostile country that they could take nothing for granted. Even now the Indians could be watching them, so once the sun burst over the eastern rims they kept to the timbered stretches alongside the wagon trail.

It was a slower ride now, weaving between towering conifers, following the wagon marks. Some of the wagons along this trail must be big, heavy Conestoga ones because many of the wheel ruts were deep. He saw one discarded axle and two bent wheels thrown into pine needles.

As he rode, Clay watched the sky.

It was just before noon when he reined his chestnut and pointed north-west.

'Smoke,' Clay said. 'Other side of that bare ridge.'

'Yeah, I see it,' Sam said, squinting at the grey wisps curling languidly into the azure sky. 'Cooking fire smoke, I reckon, but too much for one fire.'

He added, 'Could be Red Claw's village.'

Clay said, 'We'll ride and find out.'

They kept to the timber, following the Muskrat River and the wagon tracks as they wound together towards a gap in the ridge. By now the river had become shallower, gleaming in the sunlight as it tumbled over rock and shale. Here the trail was well-worn, hugging the river bank. Clay and Sam slowed their horses as the gap loomed ahead, a thin passage where the Muskrat River and the trail looked to come together, just wide enough to squeeze through.

Riding closer, Clay saw more smoke and a glimpse of Comanche lodges. Figuring there could well be riders coming in and out through the gap, Clay motioned Sam to a narrow eyebrow track that clung to the side of the ridge. Clay led the way to the foot of the track and began to climb. He reached the crest and with Sam right behind, he rode straight for a notch in the rock.

They slipped from their saddles, dropped to the flat ridge top and slithered like lizards towards the edge. Clutching his rifle, Clay lifted his head first as Sam wormed alongside him. A wisp of smoke curled over their heads and Sam whistled under his breath as they looked down on over a hundred Indian lodges, mostly tepees made of buffalo hides, a few larger ones built of brush-wood. There were indeed many small fires, over a dozen, but there was also a large one, glowing in a circle of stones planted right in the centre of the village. Clay saw mostly men but there were also squaws and small children.

A large totem pole, painted red as blood, had its head carved into the shape of a bear claw. It stood alone, thrust into the earth outside the largest wooden lodge.

There was no doubt this was Chief Red Claw's camp.

Sam pointed out half a dozen more hunters coming, this time from the south, bringing carcasses of dead deer. They were met by gleeful squaws who pulled the deer down from the ponies and dragged them to the big stones where they would be carved up ready to be cooked. Sam pointed out a well-constructed brush corral for the ponies, remarking this must be a permanent village, built recently on the bank of the Muskrat River. Two women were wading in the river collecting water. There was a young boy swimming and a wrinkled old man waded towards the bank with a fish wriggling on his long spear.

Clay's eyes ranged over the camp, resting on the men seated around what he figured was the council fire. As he expected, they were older men in that circle, but one of them in particular grabbed his attention. Seated cross-legged on the ground, smoking a long pipe, was a man wearing a Stetson hat. Most of the Indians wore fringed buckskin tunics and leggings but this bearded man was dressed in a black suit. When the man took the pipe from his lips and turned his head slightly, Clay knew him straight away.

'Gainsborough,' he said the name. 'Down there by that council fire.'

Sam exclaimed, 'Our undertaker! I'll be damned! What in hell's name is he doing here?'

'Well, he's not here to collect a body for a Christian burial,' Clay said wryly. 'Neither is that other white man under Red Claw's totem pole.'

Sam swore under his breath as the other white man began strolling around the camp, stopping to talk to a young squaw.

'Morgan, the Broken Bow storekeeper,' Sam said hoarsely.

121

'He's certainly changed his tune,' Clay said quietly. 'I remember a time when he wanted to hang a young Comanche boy for stealing. Now he's walking around Red Claw's camp like he owns it. I reckon, Sam, that we're looking at two of the lousy gunrunners.'

Sam shook his head, lamenting, 'Morgan, I can believe. He's a lousy, money-hungry bastard who'd sell his own mother for a dime or even less. But Gainsborough – well, he acts so flaming holy. If the preacher's out of town, he reads from the Good Book and says prayers when he buries folks in Boot Hill.'

'You said it, Sam,' Clay said, 'he acts holy, but like Morgan, he's a traitor.'

'There must be others,' Sam suggested. 'The likes of Morgan and Gainsborough wouldn't be able to operate a gunrunning outfit on their own.'

'Take a close look at that camp corral,' Clay directed.

Sam shielded his eyes from the sun.

'Reckon there are dozens of Comanche pinto ponies in that corral . . .' He frowned. 'But I can also see five, maybe six, well-fed horses with leather saddles on them. Holy Moses! They're white men's horses sure enough.'

Clay raised his eyes north, just beyond the limits of Red Claw's camp.

That's when he spotted the wagons.

They were half-concealed in a hollow near where the Muskrat River gushed out of a canyon and flowed past the camp. From their elevated ridge top, Clay made out men in the canyon, distant figures walking between the wagons and the river.

'We'll take a look in that canyon,' Clay decided.

'Reckon some of those men are whites,' Sam observed.

'Something's going on there, that's for sure,' Clay said.

They eased themselves back over the bare ridge to the notch where their horses were waiting.

Clay and Sam remounted and headed slowly down the thin knife-edge trail to the flat. Keeping to a line of tall, shadowy pines, they rode across the mouth of the gap, then forded the river.

Once on the other bank, they spotted a couple of Comanche hunters returning from the eastern mesa. Hastily, they edged their mounts into some sheltering willows. There they waited, concealed by the trailing willow branches, while the hunters rode past them to the Muskrat's bank. Finally, the Comanche bucks made their ponies splash through the shallows into the gap on their way to Red Claw's camp.

After they were gone, Clay signalled Sam and they left the willows and followed the rest of the rock ridge that curved around the southern side of the Comanche village. Here the ridge began to crumble and break up. Boulders littered the grass. Patches of sagebrush clung to the track. After rounding a big boulder, the two scouts made their way to a sandstone crest.

Here they were on the far side of Red Claw's camp, looking down on three wagons making a motionless line along this side of the Muskrat River.

There were no Indians below them, just two white men and one lean, rat-faced Mexican, who was lazily smoking a thin cigar while he straddled a log.

Sam recognized him immediately. 'Well, I'll be damned!'

'You know him?'

'Gringo Martinez, our town gravedigger,' Shoshone Sam said under his breath. 'Works for Gainsborough.'

'He's a long way from town.'

'And like Gainsborough, he's not here to collect corpses for burial,' Sam said grimly.

The two other men were up to their knees wading in the shallow water. Both held shiny metal pans and right now they were both examining the silt and gravel they'd just scooped out of the stream.

'Panning for gold,' Sam said hoarsely.

'Right here plumb next to Red Claw's camp and deep in hostile Comanche Territory,' Clay said softly. He surmised grimly, 'I reckon we know now what the deal is. Guns for gold.'

Sam asked incredulously, 'You mean this ornery gun-running outfit supplies rifles to Red Claw and in return they get to pan as much gold as they like?'

'That's exactly what I mean,' Clay confirmed. He added, 'And we can be damn sure these snakes prospect enough gold to make the whole arrangement worthwhile.'

'See that tall galoot examining his pan?' Sam pointed out.

'I see him,' Clay said. 'By the grin on his face, it looks like he's found a nugget.'

'He's Jake Carter, lives in Settler Creek too, same as the gravedigger! Works part-time as a bartender in Wolf Lonegan's Soiled Dove Saloon.'

Clay recognized the other prospector panning for gold. He was Rob Trapp, the red-haired, cigar-puffing saloon owner from Broken Bow. Like Morgan, the storekeeper in his town, Trapp looked to be part of this gang of traitorous gunrunners. He thought back to Burgan's attempt to ambush him after he'd left Broken Bow. He figured Burgan must have been in with them too. Seemingly it was a well-organised gang with members in both Broken Bow and Settler Creek. Clay felt a tide of anger surge inside him.

The men who worked for this outfit had no scruples. They were supplying rifles to a hothead like Chief Red Claw, knowing full well his renegade Comanches were using those weapons to butcher innocent settlers – and they were doing it out of sheer greed for gold.

But what could he and Sam do about it?

They were just two men out here alone in hostile territory.

He felt the urge to level his rifle and gun down all three of the men panning for gold but what good would that do? It would only bring every Comanche warrior in that camp down around their necks. He imagined Gainsborough, Morgan and any other white renegades in Red Claw's camp would merely stand by and watch them being scalped.

Maybe the most sensible thing to do was slip away quietly, ride to Fort Adobe and fetch some help. A column of heavily armed, blue-coated cavalrymen would be mighty handy right now.

Suddenly, the silence was shattered by a harsh command.

'Freeze! Both of you, freeze!'

The rasping voice came from right behind them, so did a second one, cold and slow and deadly. 'Do it now or we shoot to kill.'

Clay turned his head and saw Fisher and Horn standing either side of the big boulder. The former trooper Fisher and the hairy-faced prospector Horn, two men Sheriff Lonegan had offered to release from their duties to join Clay's mission, both had their rifles steady, aimed and ready to fire. Clay knew from his army days that Trooper

Fisher had been a crack shot but he wasn't sure about Horn. However, this wasn't a time to take chances.

Fisher commanded, 'Empty your saddles.'

'Nice and slow,' Horn warned.

'One damn fool move and you're both in hell,' Fisher snapped.

'Do like they say,' Clay murmured to Sam.

'Yeah,' Sam agreed reluctantly, 'they have the drop on us.'

Slowly, the two scouts dismounted and while they did, Fisher and Horn strode closer, so close they had Clay and Sam at point-blank range.

'Step away from your horses,' Fisher ordered them.

'Now!' Horn yelled.

Clay and Sam took two paces forward.

Just one more step and those guns would be poking into their chests.

'Quenah! Pahayoko!' Fisher called out.

The traitors held Clay and Sam at gunpoint as the first two Comanche warriors, then three more, leapt out from where they'd been concealed among the rocks.

'They're all yours,' Horn yelled out to the five Indians.

Within moments the Comanches sprang at the two scouts.

A heavy wooden club smashed into the left side of Clay's head, then as he fell, he was dealt another savage blow on the back of his shoulders. Almost blacking out as pain raced through his body, Clay crashed headlong to the dust. Moments later Sam joined him, collapsing into a crumpled heap, his face a heaving mask of flowing blood where a sharp Comanche knife had slashed across his left cheek.

Whooping, two Indians used their long Springfield

rifles to prod the prisoners as they lay sprawled on the ground while Horn and Fisher crouched down and relieved the two scouts of their guns.

Then the Indian named Quenah, who was tall, long-haired and lithe, issued a sharp order. Responding, the other Indians grabbed Clay and Sam, hauling them back on their feet. Battered, dazed, racked by pain, the prisoners could hardly stand. In fact, Sam's knees buckled and he had to cling to Clay to stay upright. Clay held him steady. Senses reeling, Clay saw two bucks brandish ropes with nooses already tied. For a moment Clay thought they were going to be hanged from the towering pine by the big boulder because the ropes were pulled down over the prisoners' heads and nooses tightened so brutally they sank into their necks.

But there wasn't going to be a neck-tie party.

Not yet, anyway.

Instead, the Indians yanked hard on their ropes, forcing the prisoners to stumble forward. Smirking, Fisher and Horn shouldered their rifles, gripped the bridles of the scouts' horses and sauntered ahead of the others down the grassy track that led towards the Comanche camp.

Forced to walk, Clay and Sam were jabbed with rifles and a razor-sharp spear held by a young Comanche brave. They were pushed and prodded past two large mounds of earth infested with big red ants. Seeing the captives approaching, a Comanche dressed in an army tunic and pants began to beat on the skin surface of his drum, the deep throbbing sound summoning warriors and squaws alike.

Even the old men around the council fire rose to their feet as the two white scouts were shoved to the edge of the camp.

The drumming rose to a crescendo.

Watched by the Indians, the two army scouts were marched between tepees and small cooking fires, past a bunch of younger bucks who taunted them, right up to the glowing council fire where the Comanche elders stood in silence watching.

Gainsborough and Morgan were together alongside the totem pole.

The undertaker had his arms folded while Morgan's face wore a broad grin as Clay and Sam were shoved around the edges of the big fire. Tamed coyotes and Indian camp dogs slunk up to sniff them and growl. A small boy poked both captives with a sharp stick. An ancient squaw spat at them.

'Knew you were on your way,' Gainsborough greeted them sardonically, folding his arms across his puny chest. He grinned. 'Welcome to Chief Red Claw's village.'

'He's made you welcome too,' Clay said coldly.

'Well, why not?' Morgan laughed. He added proudly, 'After all, we're business partners.'

Sam exploded, 'Goddamn traitors!'

'Reckon this crazy, loud-mouthed loon needs a pistol-whipping,' Morgan sneered, lifting a Colt .45 with his left hand.

'Hold it, Buck.' Gainsborough restrained him from striking Sam, whose shirt was now soaked with blood dripping from his cut face. 'I'm sure Red Claw's braves will take care of both of them the Comanche way. Not that we'll be around to watch the sport. We'll all be home enjoying ourselves in the saloon while these two damn fools get what's coming to them.'

'Enjoying ourselves with women too,' Morgan said. He added, 'I rather like the look of that filly you brought into my store in Broken Bow, Coleman. A couple of Triple D hands told me Old Man Drury prevented his blue-eyed boy Thomas from getting hitched to her, so that means she's free and in Settler Creek.' He chuckled. 'Might look her up and have myself some fun.'

Clay exploded, 'You lay hands on her and—'

'And you'll do nothing, Coleman,' Gainsborough said mockingly. 'By the time Buck Morgan gets around to having his fun with her, you'll be buzzard bait.'

Right then the drum fell silent.

The big, imposing figure of Red Claw filled the entrance to his lodge. Once lean and rangy like a starving wolf, the renegade Comanche chief had put on many pounds. Now he was taller, broader, his arms and legs thicker. He had a prominent aquiline nose, thick lips and a protruding chin. Bear claws sewn onto leather made a chain around his neck. Below this chain was a deep black scar running across his naked chest.

Chief Red Claw walked slowly towards the captives.

The sneer forming on his face betrayed his utter contempt.

He addressed Clay first in the halting English he'd learned during one year in a Mormon Mission School. 'I remember you – Scout Coleman – we met at the council fire – deep in the Mountains of the Moon. You were guest of Comanche Nation then. Now you are our prisoner.'

'We had a good talk at that council fire,' Clay reminded him. 'And I'm still willing to talk.'

'But the time for talking is past,' Chief Red Claw said. There was venom in his tone now. 'Paleface Gainsborough and my other white friends have told me why you are in Comanche Territory.'

'Both of us have been sent by the United States Army,'

Clay asserted. 'The army wants peace between Indians and settlers. The more rifles these white traitors supply you, the more likely there will be war.'

Red Claw loomed closer to Clay Coleman. 'And I, Chief Red Claw, want war. Even now other Comanche chiefs are riding to talk in a big meeting. Soon all the Comanche Nation will be with me. We will of course not attack the towns where our paleface friends who give us guns live – but others will be attacked – and their houses will be burned to the ground.'

An older warrior, whose long grey hair fell like string over his bony shoulders, came forward and exchanged words with Gainsborough.

The undertaker in turn spoke quietly to Red Claw.

'You, Clay Coleman, killed our friend Henderson,' the renegade chief accused. 'Brown Otter saw you shoot him dead in Rattlesnake Pass.'

Clay glanced at the old warrior and remembered. After he'd killed Henderson, he'd exchanged gunfire with two Comanche riders. He'd shot one but this grey-haired warrior, who he now knew as Brown Otter, had fled over the ledge into the night.

'Paleface Henderson was good friend to Red Claw,' the Comanche chief said. 'Very good friend.'

'Might as well tell you now because you won't be alive to tell any tales,' Gainsborough spoke up. 'Most of our rifles come from the south but this was a special consignment from east of the Plains. Henderson was bringing them to Chief Red Claw on the wagon train he was scouting for.'

'And putting the lives of innocent emigrants at risk,' Clay said.

Gainsborough shrugged. 'You're quite a preacher, Coleman.'

'You the boss of this outfit?' Clay demanded.

The undertaker hesitated. 'I know what Chief Red Claw has in store for you, so since you'll not be leaving this village alive, it'll do no harm to spill everything.' He grinned. 'We all work for Mr Wolf Lonegan, the esteemed new sheriff of Settler Creek.' Then he joked, 'So, army scouts, now you know.' He mocked, 'Mission accomplished. Well, almost.'

Red Claw sentenced the two prisoners. 'Tomorrow you die. You die slow, very slow.'

The chief signalled to four of his warriors.

The men ran forward as the drumming resumed. Two of the braves grabbed the ropes hanging from the captives' necks, others prodded the prisoners with knives and spears, pushing them towards a brush lodge less than twenty paces from the council fire.

They were shoved inside and thrown to the bare earth floor.

The Comanche braves crouched over them.

First they roped Clay's wrists together, then his ankles. Turning to Sam, they turned him over so his bloody face was in the earth. They lashed his hands behind his back, then his ankles.

One of the braves, slightly built, with thin, bloodless lips, lingered before joining the others outside.

He spoke a single word in the Comanche tongue.

'What did he say?' Sam asked. When Clay said nothing, he insisted, 'You heard him, so what did he say?'

'Ants,' Clay told him finally.

CHAPTER NINE

It was coming on noon and the high sun burned the Comanche camp. Trussed up on the ground inside the lodge, Clay tried vainly to pull his hands free but with every strain and every movement, the ropes only bit deeper into his wrists and ankles, drawing traces of blood. Sam was doing the same thing and he too felt the ropes tighten even more over his skin and bones.

Neither of them talked about that word Clay had heard, but it was on their minds. The Comanches had some special ways of killing and staking prisoners over ant hills was one of them. If this was to be their fate, then big red ants would crawl all over them, invading their noses, eyes and mouths, biting, taking their time to tantalise and eat flesh. It was a terrible way to die and it could take days. However, as an army scout, Clay had seen both sides of the cruelty coin. Some white settlers had committed atrocities too, ruthlessly burning peaceful Indian villages so they could steal their land, sometimes butchering women and children.

He lifted his head as the sound of creaking wagons came to them.

A skin flap decorated with drawings of Comanche warriors hung down over the entrance to the lodge, blocking out daylight, but there were still thin gaps in the brush walls and Clay managed to edge over to one and peer through a small chink. Some Comanches, mainly squaws and children, were watching too as the empty wagons were driven past the village, bouncing along the trail south that led to the deserted outpost, Fort Buffalo. Abel Gainsborough rode alone on the driver's seat of the lead wagon pulled by four horses. Next came Morgan and the Mexican behind the reins of the two horses hauling the second, smallest wagon while bringing up the rear was the big, lumbering Conestoga driven by Trapp and Carter. There were six horses pulling this largest wagon.

Clay noted that Doug Fisher and Wes Horn weren't part of this cavalcade. Maybe they'd stayed behind to fossick for gold in the Muskrat River in the hope of taking some nuggets home for themselves. Clay saw too that these traitors, both watching the departing wagons, had the guns they'd snatched from their prisoners tucked in their belts. They looked like armed pirates.

Soon the wagons were past the Comanche camp.

He glimpsed a heap of what the renegade white men had left behind – shiny new rifles, whiskey barrels, even some clothes for the squaws.

Clay looked over at Sam. There were thin slants of light coming through the chinks in the wall. They just touched Sam, who by now had managed to roll over on his back.

At least he'd stopped bleeding now but when he tried to speak, his voice was hoarse, just a rasp. Both men knew, however, that it was no use calling for a drink. It was unlikely they'd be given any water or food.

It was mid-afternoon when the old warrior, Brown Otter, entered the lodge.

He spoke bitterly in the Comanche tongue.

One of the two braves Clay had shot in Rattlesnake Pass had been his youngest son, he declared bitterly. All his other sons had been killed by bluecoats. Now he only had his squaw, who was lamenting. It would give Brown Otter great pleasure to sit day and night by the ant hills to watch Clay die, thus confirming their grisly fate. After this angry tirade, he stormed out of the lodge.

The afternoon wore on.

The prisoners could smell meat cooking over the fires. They could also smell the whiskey the gunrunners had left. Looking through the chink in the brush wall, Clay saw two older warriors sprawled drunkenly over a log. He turned his eyes on the men seated around the council fire. Chief Red Claw was standing, giving an oration. He repeatedly mentioned his 'paleface friend Wolf Lonegan'. Fisher and Horn were there. Later Fisher rose to his feet and walked over to where a group of squaws were carving up some venison. He tapped a young woman on her shoulder and she followed him meekly to a wigwam. This gunrunning outfit was fully entrenched here, part of Red Claw's people. And together with Sam, Clay could only sit back, watch and wait.

With sundown came clouds, making dusk arrive early.

The Comanches gathered around their cooking fires, eating and drinking.

The throbbing drumbeat sounded, slow, deep and ominous.

Darkness enfolded the Indian camp and because the cloud bank made a blanket over the moon and stars, the only light came from the glowing coals of cooking fires. Inside the lodge, it was close to pitch dark. The night wore on. Brown Otter sat guard outside the prisoners' lodge while most of the Indians returned to their wigwams.

The drumming died away.

Silence settled over Red Claw's village.

It was the midnight hour.

By now most of the fires were mere sparks in the dark.

Clay heard the distant baying of a wolf pack.

Suddenly, there was a footfall outside the lodge. It was soft and furtive. A bronze hand edged the skin flap aside. Clay glimpsed another hand, this one holding a long knife, its sharp blade silhouetted against the last glowing embers of the council fire. For a moment Clay thought it was Brown Otter but then he saw the hand loom closer. It was a lean hand, not the veined, wrinkled hand of an old man. The skin flap fell back into place and the man crouched over him. Just the faintest glow from a dying fire came through a chink and played over the Indian with the knife.

Instantly, Clay knew him.

He was older, into his twenties, more mature and his skin had hardened but Clay remembered him sure enough.

'Isatai!' Clay whispered in the stillness between them.

'Yes, it is I, Isatai,' the warrior confirmed, speaking very slowly and softly, almost under his breath in the Comanche tongue. 'I saw them bring you in.'

Isatai leaned closer, his knife close to Clay's neck.

'Red Claw intends to kill you. However, many moons ago, you save Isatai's life. Now I save yours.'

Wasting no time, the bronze-skinned Comanche reached behind Clay's back and with a single quick deft slice, cut the ropes that held his wrists. Then he turned and found the ropes that were knotted securely around the white man's ankles. He sliced through the fibres of the strong rope and Clay's ankles, like his wrists, sprang apart.

'You wish your friend to go free?'

'Sure I do.'

'The saints be praised,' Sam said fervently.

Isatai handed the knife to Clay, who instantly slashed the two sets of rope that had secured Shoshone Sam.

'Listen, Paleface Coleman,' Isatai said as the two white men rubbed their hands together to restore circulation. 'When Isatai leaves you, slide outside like silent snakes, your bellies flat on the ground. Slide past Brown Otter, who now snores like a pig. Slide out of village. You will see tall tree by corral. Your two horses are tied there. They are saddled. There are two new rifles by the tree, both are loaded.'

'I owe you, Isatai,' Clay said.

'No, you do not owe me and now Isatai does not owe you,' the Indian stated firmly. 'Isatai has repaid his debt. But before you go, hear this, Paleface Coleman. Once you ride away, you are my enemy. If we meet in battle, Isatai will kill you.'

'I know what you're saying, Isatai,' Clay said, adding, 'but I hope we do not meet in battle.'

The Comanche stood up. Unlike the boy of sixteen years, he had grown tall, almost as tall as Clay.

'Isatai hopes this too.'

'You'll make a fine chief one day,' Clay predicted.

Just the faintest hint of a smile curled the Indian's lips. 'That is what Long Knife told me.'

'So you're in with Chief Long Knife?'

'His daughter, Prairie Rose, is Isatai's squaw.'

Then Isatai was gone.

Clutching the Comanche's knife, Clay dropped flat to the ground. He lifted the skin flap and glanced out over the camp. Brown Otter was sleeping on his left side, facing

136

away from him. True to Isatai's description, he was snoring like a pig. Clay saw the lean figure of Isatai glide past the smoking remains of the council fire and disappear inside a wigwam.

Turning his head, Clay motioned Sam to follow him. He wormed right out of the lodge, slithered past a wigwam that was wreathed in darkness, then slid on his chest and belly between two brush lodges. A mangy coyote that had become relatively tame after scrounging discarded meat in the Comanche camp stood up on the other side of the council fire.

Sam swore as the lean animal padded their way, making yipping noises.

Still the coyote came closer, sniffing the ground, then howling like a wolf as it saw Sam flat to the ground.

'Give me the knife,' Sam demanded.

The coyote howled loudly now, rousing others who were bedded around the smouldering fires. Clay saw one Comanche, then another, emerge from wigwams. Swiftly, Sam slit the animal's throat and it sank into the grass. For a moment silence gripped Red Claw's camp. The two white men lay like stones as the two Indians spoke together. One Comanche warrior walked towards the river, but the other stalked towards the prisoners' lodge, where Brown Otter was still leaning against the brush wall fast asleep.

Within moments the whole camp would know the captives had escaped.

'We're getting the hell out of here,' Clay told Sam.

They jumped to their feet and plunged into the night, running around the edge of the Comanche village. There was enough light from dying fires to show Indian warriors pouring out of their wigwams. Suddenly a shout of fury came from the prisoners' lodge. The angry young Indian who'd discovered the escape felled the sentry, Brown Otter, with a single blow for his neglect.

Clay made out the dim outline of the tall arrowhead pine tree Isatai had told them about. The fugitives slashed their way through tall grass and sagebrush. Clay made the tree first. True to Isatai's word, Clay's chestnut, Rusty, and Sam's bay were tethered to the pine trunk. Both horses were saddled. Before mounting, Clay grabbed the two Springfield rifles leaning against the tree. He tossed one to Sam, who caught it as he reached his horse. Clay was first in the saddle. He saw half a dozen braves come running their way. Fisher was with them, yanking up his pants as he ran. Then came Wes Horn, yelling out that these escaping prisoners needed to be filled with lead. Moments later a furious Chief Red Claw emerged from his lodge, urging his warriors to run down the escaping prisoners.

Secured to Clay's saddle-horn was a small cloth bag. It smelled of gunpowder. Knowing these rifles each had a single shot in the locker, Isatai had probably given them powder and bullets. There was no time to check because a barrage of shots rang out from the camp and one bullet thudded into the pine just a whisker from Sam's left ear.

Leaning over in the saddle, Clay used Isatai's knife to slash the ropes that were strung across the corral's entrance. Scared by the gunfire, the Indian ponies began milling, then stampeding around the corral.

The two fugitives headed their horses west into the darkness.

Behind them, Red Claw's camp was erupting.

Comanche warriors raced to the corral as some of the spooked ponies fled.

Clay and Sam kept riding hard, thundering over a grassy flat.

Reaching the far side, they drew their horses under a sheltering rock ledge. Mercifully, till now, there was no moonlight, making it difficult for the Indians to pursue them but Clay noted the clouds were moving on and stars were beginning to show.

'We'll circle south,' Clay decided.

'That'll take us to the wagon trail,' Sam pointed out.

'We won't ride the trail because it could be lousy with Red Claw's renegades,' Clay said. 'We'll just ride close to the trail, slow and careful.'

'If we go all the way, it'll take us to Fort Buffalo,' Sam said, frowning.

'It's about time we had a good look around there.'

'Don't forget, these Springfield rifles are single shots,' Sam reminded him. 'If we run into trouble we'll have one chance and one only.' He confirmed Clay's hopes. 'Your Comanche friend gave me a bag, same as you, only I've had a look inside mine. Five spare bullets and just enough powder to fire them.'

They heard Comanches calling to each other in the night.

A big ghostly moon glowed through the thinning clouds.

Clay nudged the chestnut forward and the two riders clung to the ledge as it led further away from Red Claw's camp. They reached a creek that flowed into the Muskrat River. Clay led the way across, swiftly flowing water lashing his stirrups. Less than a minute later they were on the other side of the creek.

Suddenly, they glimpsed four warriors running swiftly across the grassy flat. Moments later they saw a Comanche

139

riding bareback on one of the pinto ponies that hadn't escaped from the corral.

The two scouts drew their horses into a shallow hollow, waiting in silence as the Indians came closer.

Both Clay and Sam lifted their rifles.

They heard the Comanche rider yell out to the other bucks. One young warrior crested the hollow but then kept moving. Clay and Sam stayed motionless in the darkness as the sounds of voices and hoofs were lost on the rising wind. Swiftly, the fugitives left the hollow, riding between pines, then into a canyon.

They rode all night, keeping to the higher ridges and slopes just west of the Muskrat River and the wagon trail that clung to its banks. Red Claw's Comanche warriors were scouring the country for the escaped captives. Twice Clay saw Indians on the trail and once Sam glimpsed them fording the river. Two hours after midnight a bunch of bucks came close to the ridge the scouts were riding but then they gave up their searching, lighting a fire.

Clay and Sam just kept heading south, resting their horses twice before dawn.

Daybreak flooded Comanche Territory with new light.

Wary now, the scouts opted for timber cover.

A full day passed and no Indian sign, not even a smoke signal.

Maybe, Clay figured, Red Claw had decided the escaped prisoners had fled west for the Big Bend Country, where there was a small garrison of cavalrymen. In fact, Clay had considered this himself but instead he wanted to find out exactly what was going on in that old outpost, Fort Buffalo, where the wagons loaded with rifles seemed to come from.

Dusk clothed the forest where they'd halted their horses.

Having eaten no food since their capture, both men were hungry.

Clay watched while Sam rode stealthily down to the Muskrat.

It took Shoshone Sam just five minutes to grab a struggling beaver by the tail and kill it with Isatai's knife. Clay rubbed two sticks together. The friction caused heat, then a wisp of smoke, finally a burst of flame, which Clay applied to a pile of pine needles that had drifted between two protruding tree roots. Sheltered by berry trees and low-sweeping pine branches, a small cooking fire was safe enough here but Clay only kept it alight long enough to cook the beaver. Once they were eating the meat, he kicked earth over the fire.

Sam was so weary he nodded off to sleep. Clay let him have two hours of shuteye before nudging him awake and resuming the trail south. By daybreak they rode the rim above the ford they'd crossed two days ago. Heading down from the rim, they checked the wagon tracks.

They were very fresh.

The three wagons had passed this way only hours ago.

Clay and Sam kept to cover, still careful not to be seen.

They rode all day, shadowing the wagon trail.

It was the hour before dusk when Clay saw a glimpse of white canvas.

The two scouts had crested a timbered rise that overlooked the Muskrat River and the trail that hugged its western bank. Just ahead, less than a mile away, was the Conestoga wagon, lumbering along well behind the other two.

The riders watched for a full minute as the shadows lengthened.

The two lead wagons had drawn adjacent to where the river tumbled swiftly over some boulder-strewn rapids. The trail slewed down to a grassy plain and the battered walls of old Fort Buffalo.

The two foremost horse-drawn wagons swayed over the crest on the down trail.

These wagons were soon lost from view, leaving the heavier Conestoga on its own as it swayed laboriously towards the head of the falls.

Lifting his rifle, Clay told Sam, 'We'll ride down there now.'

CHAPTER TEN

Leaving the timber, they rode straight down to the trail, where filmy dust churned up by the passing wagons still hung like a cloud in the greying stillness. The last covered wagon was almost at the crest as Clay and Sam urged their mounts along the trail. They rode swiftly, relying on the rattling and creaking of the old Conestoga to drown out the sound of their oncoming horses.

Clay reached the big wagon first.

He slowed his chestnut, looking through its rear opening.

Trapp and Carter, the same gunrunners who'd been behind the Conestoga's team when they left Red Claw's camp, were still there now, hunched together on the driving seat. They were talking, sharing lewd jokes and Clay could smell their cigar smoke from the rear of the wagon.

Motioning Sam to ride right alongside him, Clay reached up, grabbed the swaying wagon's rear iron hoop and hauled himself out of the saddle into the Conestoga. Responding to Clay's whisper, Sam leaned over and snatched up the chestnut's trailing reins.

'Your rifle, Sam,' Clay demanded softly.

Sam had worked too long with Clay Coleman over many years to question him so he stood in his stirrups and handed over his Springfield. He knew what he had to do next as Clay stood up, a rifle in each hand and walked stealthily and slowly over the vibrating wagon floor. Still Trapp and Carter were oblivious to his presence behind them. As they started the downhill journey to the old outpost, Trapp swore and flicked the reins to push the team into moving faster.

The wagon wheels bounced over a bed of gritty stones.

Clay crept closer till he crouched right behind them.

Suddenly he thrust the rifle muzzles hard into each spine.

'Just keep driving your wagon,' Clay said softly as Trapp and Carter froze like statues on the driving seat. He warned, 'If just one of you makes a fool move, you're both dead.'

Trapp recognized the voice before he turned his head. 'Coleman!'

Carter exclaimed hoarsely, 'How in hell's name—?'

'Save your breath,' Clay told them. Keeping his rifles steady, he called out to Sam. 'Tie the horses to the back of the wagon and come on board.'

'You're goddamn crazy,' Carter croaked.

'Whatever you're intending, you won't get away with it,' Trapp snarled.

Clay commanded, 'Button your lip till you're spoken to.'

He heard the thump of Sam's body on the wagon floor as he scrambled into the back of the Conestoga.

Snatching a quick look between the two gunrunners, Clay saw the other wagons at the foot of the slope, both ready to roll across the flat to the crumbling walls of the old abandoned outpost. Then he glimpsed one extra wagon down there, this one standing just inside the gaping entrance.

Sam tramped across the wagon floor and crouched next to Clay.

'Take their guns,' Clay told him.

'With pleasure.'

'You'll pay for this – both of you,' Trapp said grimly.

Sam reached out and lifted two Peacemaker Colts from Trapp's twin holsters, then grabbed Carter's single Colt .45. Next he groped between them and picked up the rifle that lay at their boots.

'Keep driving the wagon,' Clay said, keeping the rifle muzzles hard in their backs.

'Nice and steady,' Sam commanded.

'I'll take one of those Peacemakers,' Clay told Sam.

'I'm just checking it's loaded. Yep, sure is.' Sam hummed as he slipped the gun into Clay's holster. 'All ready in your leather.' He examined the other Peacemaker. 'This one's for me. Fully loaded, like yours. I'll put the Colt in my belt.' He even afforded a chuckle. 'Now I don't feel naked any more.'

By now the other two moving wagons were halfway across the grassy flat, their horses slowing as they approached the fort. That's when Clay saw a thick-set man dressed in black – Stetson, shirt, pants and boots – saunter out of the outpost and stand with arms folded waiting to greet them. The man's face was in shadow under the wide brim of his hat.

'Who is he?' Clay demanded.

'You'll find out soon enough, just before you go to hell,' Trapp replied.

Clay said coldly, 'Well, Trapp, you'll be in hell yourself

if you don't give me a straight answer before I count to three. One, two—'

Trapp sweated. 'Damn you!'

'He's Frank Logan,' Carter said quickly.

Clay drew in his breath.

He demanded, 'Trader Logan who hangs out in Fort Adobe?'

'Yeah, that's him,' Trapp admitted.

'Didn't he get hitched to Major Keating's daughter?' Sam asked.

'That's right,' Clay confirmed.

He was thinking that a man like Logan, being close to but not exactly part of the military, would be in a prime position to know gun suppliers.

'So what the hell is he doing out here?' Sam grunted.

'We might just ask him,' Clay said grimly. 'That's unless we put a bullet between his eyes before we do any talking. Reckon I know Trader Logan better than you, Sam, and that's not just because I tangled with him. He was slippery as a wet snake when I knew him at Fort Adobe and he's obviously the same now.'

Trader Logan sauntered over to greet the drivers of the two wagons that had just come to a standstill by the outpost's entrance. Gainsborough climbed out of his wagon first, then his Mexican gravedigger jumped to the ground next, finally followed by Morgan. By now the Conestoga had reached the foot of the slope and was creaking and swaying over the flat where the three gun-runners were waiting for them in the gathering dusk.

With their guns ready, Clay and Sam crouched lower now, directly behind the men in the driving seat. Their wagon rolled closer. They could hear voices. Although he'd never worn a uniform, Frank Logan was giving sharp orders like an officer, a man who expected to be obeyed. In contrast, Abel Gainsborough's tone was sermonic and the Mexican said nothing.

'Take this wagon right up to them and halt the horses just where they're waiting,' Clay said quietly.

Trapp's sweat flowed down to his neck and Carter whimpered like a scared dog as the horses slowed to a walk and the fort entrance loomed ever closer in the fading light. One of the lead horses snorted when the Conestoga came to a shuddering halt, right beside the three waiting men who were so close they could almost touch the wagon.

Keeping his rifle aimed at Trapp, Clay reared suddenly to his feet with the Peacemaker in his right hand. Sam stood up beside him as Trader Logan, Gainsborough and the Mexican, speechless and incredulous in the sudden silence, simply stared at them.

'It wasn't our fault – we were jumped,' Carter blubbered.

'They snuck up on us,' Trapp explained.

'The first man to slap leather gets a bullet,' Clay warned. 'We'll start with you, Trader Logan. Lower your right hand, nice and slow-like, lift that army pistol you're wearing and then let it drop to the ground.'

'Listen, Coleman,' Logan didn't speak in his usual clipped, arrogant voice. His tone was softer now, persuasive. 'This is a time to act sensible, fellas. We make big money working for Wolf Lonegan, who owns this outfit.' He emphasised slowly, 'Real big money. All of us will be rich men, yes, rich.' Smiling now, showing a row of gleaming white teeth, he tempted, 'Why don't you join us, Clay Coleman? You too, Sam. Both of you would be rich for the rest of your lives.'

147

'Go to hell,' Clay said bluntly.

The trader began to stammer now, 'Mr Lonegan's – a reasonable man – I'm sure he'd be more than happy to have both of you gents on his payroll. What do you say?'

'I say this, Logan,' Clay said coldly. 'Empty that holster or you're dead.'

Sweating, Logan edged his hand downwards. Shaking fingers fastened around his gun handle. Inch by inch he began to lift the army pistol clear of its holster.

But then, suddenly, surprisingly, it was Abel Gainsborough who swooped for his gun. Seeing the move, Clay turned his Peacemaker on the crafty mortician and fired two bullets in rapid succession. The impact of Clay's slugs lifted Gainsborough clean off his feet but the diversion was enough to spur Logan into taking a desperate risk. Instead of dropping his army pistol, he jerked it upwards. Sam's first bullet burned into his chest. Dead on his feet, he collapsed beside Gainsborough. That's when Trapp took a chance and threw himself over the rear horses harnessed to the Conestoga wagon. Terrified, the two geldings reared in unison, throwing Trapp to the ground, where their iron-shod hoofs stamped him into the dust. Trapp tried frantically to claw his way up, demanding help from Carter, who responded by grabbing hold of Sam's rifle and wrenching it from him. Still crouching, Clay shot Carter at point-blank range. Dead in a blink of an eye, Carter crashed over the wagon's rocking floor just as Trapp sank back into the blood-flecked dust.

'The greaser's running,' Sam warned, lifting his gun.

The terrified Mexican gravedigger's sombrero flew into the air as he fled frantically into the dusk.

'Let him live, he won't hurt us,' Clay restrained his friend.

Agreeing, Sam lowered his gun.

Neither of them would rest easy shooting a fugitive in the back.

'It's a helluva long way to the Rio Grande,' Sam remarked as the Mexican vanished into the darkness. 'A month or more on foot, I reckon. He'll wear out his boots and get blisters. Serve him damn well right!'

Hearing a sudden, distant rumble, Clay looked back over his shoulder.

'Sam,' he warned sharply.

'Yeah?'

'The ridge behind us,' Clay said. 'We've got trouble – big trouble.'

Standing up and glancing at their back trail, Sam went pale, exclaiming hoarsely, 'Jumping Jeremiah! It's the whole Comanche Nation!'

'I'd say, Red Claw and his renegades,' Clay amended quietly, letting his eyes range over the big bunch of Indians who'd just topped the ridge. 'Reckon they've been trailing us from the camp and they've just heard shooting.'

'And they're about to head down here—' Sam cried, scrambling to the back of the wagon where he'd tied his horse next to Rusty. 'We'll need to make ourselves real scarce!'

Clay joined him at the rear wagon hoop.

Right at that moment, the last glow of sundown caught half a dozen warriors ahead of the rest riding their painted ponies to the head of the trail. They were bunched together behind a lean Comanche brandishing his rifle. It was then Clay caught a fleeting glimpse of the Indian right behind him.

'Sam, see that rider out in front.'

149

'Thin as a rake with long hair?'

Clay lifted his rifle. 'That's the one. Take him now.'

'I'll try,' Sam said, drawing a bead on the foremost Indian.

Sam fired and hit him high in his ribcage. The thin Comanche swayed in his cloth saddle and pitched sideways, exposing the rider behind him, Red Claw. Clay knew he had one fleeting chance, only one. As he pulled his trigger, the rifle bucked against his shoulder. Clay's bullet struck the renegade chief high in his chest and he slumped over his pony's head. Red Claw screamed, then tried to clutch his pinto's flowing mane before dropping and hitting the dirt.

'Get the hell out of here,' Clay said.

They both untethered their mounts and leapt into their saddles.

Without even looking over their shoulders, they rode their horses east into the beckoning darkness.

It was late afternoon when they saw the distant wisps of smoke curling from the cooking stoves of Settler Creek. The riders had been in the saddle for two nights and close on two days. In fact, Clay Coleman and Shoshone Sam had ridden almost non-stop, halting only to rest and feed their horses briefly, but giving them a longer spell earlier today around sun up at Bitter Springs. There they'd found Scout Charlie Warren and his half-dozen bluecoats, all well away from Major Keating's eagle eye and sleeping off last night's visit to the ramshackle saloon. At least Warren's one-eyed cook sobered up enough to fry them hash and eggs and make them coffee.

Not wasting any time, Clay and Sam had ridden out within the hour.

Now, after a full day's hard riding, they came to where the Bitter Springs track joined the main emigrant trail into Settler Creek.

Sundown was blood red across the western sky as they reached town limits. Most of the gunrunners had been killed and Clay assumed Red Claw too was dead. But had this news reached Wolf Lonegan yet? Or was he blissfully unaware his gunrunning outfit was virtually destroyed and the game was up? Clay figured that if Lonegan knew, he would either stay here, waiting, intent on destroying the two scouts who had the evidence on him – or he would ride hell for leather out of town, maybe clean out of the territory. Snakes like Wolf Lonegan were quite adept at starting up again.

That's why he had to be brought to justice before that happened.

He could be captured and taken to the fort to be dealt with but Clay was in no mood to play things by the book.

Settler Creek looked almost deserted, hardly a soul on Main Street.

Not that this was unusual. Mostly the townsfolk would be home eating their evening meals and it was a bit early for cowboys from nearby spreads to be arriving for a night of drinking in the saloons. Wolf's General Emporium had shut early and there was only a single light burning in the Soiled Dove Saloon. Clay decided first they needed to check on the womenfolk, so they turned down Black Deuce Alley. Maybe Kymana and Abigale had heard talk about Lonegan.

They turned by the Black Deuce Saloon and rode down the alley.

A lamp had been lit inside Doc Brock's surgery.

An oldster sat in the open doorway of the next-door

cabin, ignoring his wife's summons for supper. As they rode further down, most of the alley was wreathed in shadow, maybe because the last crimson slash of sunset provided a semblance of light. Approaching the creek, Clay noticed that in contrast to the preacher's house, Sam's cabin seemed to have no lamp burning. There was obviously some sort of meeting at the preacher's manse because light spilled from his front windows and a black-hooded carriage with two horses in harness stood outside the white picket fence.

The two scouts rode right up to Sam's cabin.

The front door was ajar.

Clay dismounted quickly and opened the door wide.

The cabin was in darkness but the wood stove was still alight and the coffee pot was rattling on its hot plate, steam rising. Sam ran to join Clay as he lit the wall lamp. Its flickering light showed them an upturned chair, the table on its side and broken plates on the ground, all signs of a struggle.

'What's happened? Where are they?' Sam cried despairingly.

'Scout around outside,' Clay told him, looking out through the window. 'Meanwhile, I'll check with the folks I can see leaving the preacher's house. Maybe someone's seen or heard something.'

Clay loped across the alley just as Tom Drury and widow Avis Whitely walked up the preacher's path towards their waiting carriage. He reached Drury as he was helping the widow up on to the front seat.

'Drury, we need your help,' Clay said.

'I've just taken Widow Whitely here to make wedding arrangements,' Tom Drury explained their presence quickly. 'My father considered there was no reason to delay, especially since Avis, I mean Widow Whitely, is staying under our ranch roof. Folks do talk, you know—'

'Drury, you've been here, right opposite Sam's place,' Clay interrupted. 'You must have seen what happened.'

'Well, yes,' Drury admitted.

The rancher's son hesitated, struggling within himself. He was remembering his father had always taught him a man should mind his own nose and not get involved in things that don't concern him.

'Thomas,' the widow said sternly, 'what happened is none of our business.'

'For once make your own damn decision,' Clay advised Drury bluntly.

The rancher's son swallowed and then decided, 'Yes, yes, I will.' He admitted, 'We did see what happened. We came here half an hour ago and saw Sheriff Lonegan and two deputies, Doug Fisher and Wesley Horn, arresting the womenfolk in that cabin. The women put up a fight but then the law officers took out their guns so Sam's squaw and Miss Abigale Wyatt surrendered. I have no idea what was their misdemeanour. I assumed it was disturbing the peace. Anyway, we then went inside the manse.'

Avis suggested, 'I suppose you'll find them in the town jail.'

'Maybe, but maybe not,' Sam called out. Frowning, he was studying the churned up dirt outside the cabin. 'They took them, in fact, they actually dragged them, towards the creek. Marks are plain, real plain.'

Maybe too plain, Clay figured.

He strode over to where Sam stood with his bay gelding.

'Their tracks lead to the creek and unless my ole peepers are fooling me, I reckon they start again on the other bank, heading for Amos Brindle's old barn, which

Lonegan uses for storing flour, salt, hay, you name it. No one owns it now so he doesn't have to pay a dime.' Sam declared, 'With Fisher and Horn back, that slimy sheriff sure knows everything. He knows we escaped. He figures we'll show our faces soon so that's why he took our women for hostages.'

Clay looked over the creek at the old barn steeped in fading light.

The arrests had been made in daylight, in full view of not only Drury and the widow, but probably the preacher too. Wolf Lonegan must know folks would talk and that Clay and Sam would hear that talk once they arrived in town.

'Or he's using them as bait in a trap,' Clay decided.

'Huh?'

'Lonegan, Fisher and Horn will be staked out waiting for us.'

'Bastards!' Sam cussed, running inside.

He grabbed his old double-barrelled shotgun from its wall hooks, then rejoined Clay, who was already in the saddle.

They rode behind the cabin.

Instead of crossing the creek, they stayed in the water. Concealed by willows, they kept to the middle of the creek and headed downstream until they halted in a pool adjacent to Brindle's barn. There they dismounted, tied their horses to a tall willow on the far bank, climbed out of the creek and dropped flat to the ground. Nightfall was close but they could make out a thin slant of light seeping through a crack in the old logs. The big barn door was just ajar and Clay spotted a rifle barrel protruding.

'Rode past here a few times on my way home from trapping,' Sam said, recalling, 'There's a loft on the northern

side and I reckon there's Brindle's old ladder still somewhere near the wall. Mind you, it could be broken.'

'We'll take a closer look,' Clay said.

They dropped to the ground.

With their bodies flat to the grass and dirt, they began
to worm their way inch by inch towards the barn. Clay
glimpsed horses tethered to a leaning tie rail. He heard a
coyote's call as the sun drifted below the western rims.
Low voices drifted to them from inside the barn.

'Sam, I'll try to climb up to the loft,' Clay said softly.
'You get as close to that front door as you can and get
ready to bust inside if shooting starts.'

'Watch that goddamn ladder,' Sam warned as Clay
began crawling towards the north wall.

Five minutes later Clay found the ladder half concealed
in long grass.

It was ancient, rickety, with half its rungs missing but
when Clay lifted it up, its top reached the loft door. He
placed his left boot on the first rung. Splinters of wood
flew off and the ladder sagged against the wall under his
weight. He now planted his right boot on the same rung.
He heard a gentle crackle but the rung held. There was no
second or third rung but the fourth was firm enough for
him to put pressure on and he levered himself up there.
The next rung was fine, then there were two missing. He
hauled himself over the space and grabbed the highest
rung, which was just below the loft door. Slowly, carefully,
he lifted himself up level with the loft door. He eased his
fingers under the door and pulled gently. The loft door
creaked on its iron hinges but Clay prised it open enough
for him to wedge his two elbows on the timber and heave
himself on to the upper wooden floor of Amos Brindle's
old barn.

There was a solitary lantern burning, hanging right over two barrels of whiskey. The light it cast was very pallid, flickering, but Clay was able to make out the two women tossed unceremoniously on the rotting wooden floor. Both were handcuffed like a couple of criminals. Fisher was beside them, sitting nonchalantly astride a hay bale. He held a Colt .45 in each hand, talking to Wes Horn who stood with his rifle just inside the big entrance door. Clay couldn't see Lonegan. Maybe he was taking it easy back in his office, leaving it all to these two hellions he'd pinned badges on.

Clay wormed closer to where the loft overlooked the rest of the barn.

There he crouched, right over bags of sugar, salt and potatoes waiting to be sold in Lonegan's store.

'After we've taken care of Coleman and Sam, we'll take care of these two women,' Fisher chuckled. He placed one gun on the hay bale and rested his free hand on Abigale's upper leg, squeezing her through her rumpled dress. 'Reckon this one might enjoy my style too.'

'Take your hand off me, swine!' Abigale yelled.

'Scream out all you like, woman,' Fisher invited. 'Make a noise! Both of you! That'll bring your men right here, into the teeth of our guns!'

Clay rose high, standing tall and dark like Nemesis on the rim of the loft. Then coldly, slowly, menacingly, he broke the sudden silence, 'You heard what she said, Fisher. Take your filthy paw off her.'

Fisher's left hand jerked up his Colt but he never aimed it because Clay's Peacemaker thundered twice, blasting him clean off the hay bale. The gunrunner staggered against boxes of merchandise marked for sale in Wolf's Emporium and pitched forward, dead before he struck the floor. Meanwhile, Horn spun around at the door, turning his rifle on Clay, but a split moment later Shoshone Sam's double-barrelled shotgun boomed like an outburst of thunder. Dozens of lead pellets peppered Horn's body and blew the twin doors wide open.

'Clay!' Abigale called out a desperate warning. 'Whiskey barrels!'

He glimpsed a furtive, shadowy movement beside the two barrels.

Crouching, Wolf Lonegan blasted a bullet into the lantern, shattering its glass into fiery fragments. Tiny flames began licking the hay bale next to the frantically screaming women as Lonegan dodged behind his merchandise crates. Clay leapt from the loft and landed on sugar bags. He ran for the burning hay bale, booting it clear of Abigale's torn dress. Taking advantage of this momentary diversion, Lonegan ran for the open door where Sam had just discarded his empty shotgun and stood fumbling for his six-shooter. Lonegan pumped two shots at Sam, one missing him, the other dropping him in the doorway where he lay yelping in pain. Moments later, Clay came at the gunrunner boss. Wolf Lonegan spun around, twin Colt .45s aimed ready to kill, but before he could fire even one, Clay's bullet blasted a hole through his heart.

Clay ran to the dead man, wrenched the handcuff keys from his belt and loped back to the prisoners, who were trying to scramble free from the rising flames. Unlocking them both, he returned to Sam, who was cussing like a trooper as he clutched his bloody right shoulder.

'We'll get him to Doc Brock's surgery,' Clay said.

They pulled him to his feet and helped him stumble through the spreading flames and swirling smoke towards their horses. Moments later, a firestorm engulfed old Amos Brindle's barn.

Major Keating had one of his rare smiles for Clay Coleman and the young woman who sat next to him in his Fort Adobe office. Lieutenant Rawlings had just brought in a tray of cookies to go with the coffee they were drinking. These two officers rarely entertained but they'd made an exception for Clay and Abigale.

'I've authorized an extra payment for you, Scout Coleman,' Keating told him. 'It's one hundred United States dollars, enough for you to share some with that old reprobate, Shoshone Sam, who apparently helped you out.'

'He's nursing a sore shoulder but he's enjoying Kymana fussing over him,' Clay related. He promised, 'I'll see he gets his share,'

'We're beholden to you, Coleman,' Major Keating admitted, sipping his coffee. 'In fact, the whole territory is. You smashed the gunrunning outfit and now there's a good chance the settlers and the Comanches can live together in peace, especially as that renegade bunch have a new chief. Scout Warren and a patrol from Bitter Creek Outpost came in an hour before you. And Warren brought some rare good news.'

'Excellent news,' Lieutenant Rawlings confirmed. He announced, 'With Red Claw's demise, there's a new chief. You know him sure enough.'

'Name's Isatai,' Keating told Clay. 'He's young, ambitious, but he says his tribe is tired of war. The men want to hunt the buffalo, the women want to settle down and raise kids.' The major conceded, with another of his rare smiles, 'I never thought I'd say this to you, but I'll say it now. Clay Coleman, you made the right decision when you saved him from that neck-tie party.'

'Amen,' Rawlings said enthusiastically. He looked straight at Clay. 'If you ever want to go back to scouting, there's a job waiting here for you.'

'Not interested,' Clay said quickly. 'Fact is, I aim to ride back to the cabin I raised in Beaver Town – and settle down.' He reached over and clasped Abigale's hand. 'Now, gentlemen, I have two questions. Is Chaplain O'Flaherty still in Fort Adobe and is he sober right now?'

'The answers to that one is, yes, he's here, and two, because it's not quite eleven in the morning there's a fighting chance he's only had a couple of glasses.'

'Fetch him,' Clay said. 'We need him to marry us.' He hesitated. 'Uh – uh – that's if Miss Abigale Wyatt will agree?'

Responding eagerly, Abigale jumped off her chair, draped herself over his knees and kissed him long and hard, so long and hard in fact that the two officers became red-faced and had to look away.

'Fetch Chaplain O'Flaherty!' Major Keating ordered his lieutenant. He roared, 'On the double!'